PRAISE FOR ALEX MASON

"It is brutal, wastes no time, and is full of action."

AMAZON REVIEW

"Better than Bond, Bourne, or Reacher."

AMAZON REVIEW

"For fans of Clancy, Mitch App, and Brad Taylor."

AMAZON REVIEW

"Same level as Patterson or Baldacci."

AMAZON REVIEW

"This book is filled with action, intrigue, espionage, and everything else lovers of a good thriller want."

AMAZON REVIEW

RUSSIAN ROULETTE

AN ALEX MASON THRILLER

DAVID ARCHER

BLAKE BANNER

RIGHTHOUSE

ISBN-13: 978-1-63696-306-8

ISBN-10: 1-63696-306-4

Cover design by: Damonza

Printed in the United States of America

www.righthouse.com

www.instagram.com/righthousebooks

www.facebook.com/righthousebooks

twitter.com/righthousebooks

ALEX MASON THRILLERS
Odin (Book 1)
Ice Cold Spy (Book 2)
Mason's Law (Book 3)
Assets and Liabilities (Book 4)
Russian Roulette (Book 5)
Executive Order (Book 6)
Dead Man Talking (Book 7)
All The King's Men (Book 8)
Flashpoint (Book 9)
Brotherhood of the Goat (Book 10)
Dead Hot (Book 11)
Blood on Megiddo (Book 12)
Son of Hell (Book 13)

PROLOGUE

José Fernandez had never known his wife to do anything remarkable. Had her life been a golf course, she would have been exactly par. She was quite pretty (she might have been beautiful if she had had some remarkable feature on her face), she had black hair and dark eyes and regular features, she was neither fat nor thin and she had all the right curves in all the right places; but not in a way you would ever notice.

Her personality was much like her looks. She was charming, never really got more than annoyed, never got depressed, was never excessively happy. She might have been adorable or fascinating, only she was never extreme enough to achieve either state. Of course that made her ideal for a job as a civil servant—a post which, in Spain, glories in the name of "functionary." The name was appropriate because that was exactly what Maria Garcia Orcera, José's wife, did at the Malaga City Hall: she functioned.

Maria had once seen a documentary on Spanish TV about the sea squirt. The narrator had described it as a creature which starts its life cycle as a predator, eventually finds a rock, or a solid place to which it attaches itself, then proceeds to eat its own brain and become a vegetable. "And in this sense," said the narrator, "it is very similar to a functionary."

That had amused her a lot, though she had not shown it.

In her professional life she never missed a day at work, she never arrived late, she never left work unfinished and never did it badly. Neither did she stay a second past three PM, nor did she produce work that was good enough to be noticed. She was, in four words, an unremarkable sea squirt.

And that was exactly what José had always loved so much about her (he being also a functionary). In fact it was what all their friends loved about her: She was utterly predictable. Which was why it was so deeply unsettling when, in early April, Maria announced that they were taking two weeks off in May. They were due the time, she told him, and she had already arranged it with both of their heads of department. And, as if this were not disturbing enough, she then compounded his dismay by turning up late after work driving a brand new Audi A4 sedan.

They had stood on the sidewalk and she had hugged him and grinned while he shook his head and looked alarmed.

"Are you crazy? How are we going to pay for it? Where are we going to park it? I already have a car. *You* have a car. You're crazy!"

She had told him not to be silly and she had kissed him a lot (which just made the whole thing even more bizarre). "I won the lottery!" she said, "I didn't tell you because I wanted it to be a surprise. I've always wanted an Audi, haven't you? And there's more!"

"Lottery? Nobody wins the lottery. More? You know I don't like surprises."

"We're going on holiday!"

"Holiday? Where? When? Why? It's not summer yet."

"May! José, I *told* you we were taking two weeks in May!"

"But I thought..." he said and went and peered into the car through the tinted windows. "I thought we'd stay at home or go to Cadiz for a week..."

"*José...!*" She made a pouting face, knowing he could never resist that. "You are spoiling everything!"

"It's just... It's unexpected. How much do we have to pay every month for this?" He opened the door and gazed at the controls.

"I *told* you! Nothing! It's paid for!"

He looked up at her and winced. "And the holiday?"

"Nothing!" She laughed. "It's paid for! Aren't you even going to ask where we're going?"

It hadn't occurred to him because he didn't really want to know. "Where?" he asked with more anxiety than curiosity. He was still hunkered down by the car door and she hunkered down beside him. He glanced at her face. Her eyes were brighter than normal and she seemed to have more teeth, and they were whiter. He had never seen her like this and was wondering if it would all lead in the end to a divorce. "We are going," she said, "*to Belarus!*"

He made a face as though his mother-in-law had just told him they were having toad's brains for dinner. It was a mix of distress and incomprehension, a kind of facial *why?*

"*Belarus?* Where is that? Isn't that near Russia? Aren't we at war with them?"

"Of course not! We are going to the beautiful city of Minsk!"

He stood. "I thought Minsk was in Russia."

"It's the capital of Belarus, between Poland, Russia and Ukraine."

"You're crazy! What's wrong with you? What's happened to you? Ukraine? We are going on holiday to a country that's between Russia and Ukraine? You're mad!"

She dismissed his anxiety with the same ease with which she dismissed almost everything about him. A brief, "Oh, come on!" was sufficient, though for good measure she added, "The war is miles away!" and illustrated this by lifting her hands, as though she were holding a map, and saying, "Look, we are here, in Minsk," and she pointed at imaginary Minsk with her finger, "And the fighting is all the way down here," she pointed to a distant spot which was presumably the southeastern area of Donbas and Mariupol.

He narrowed his eyes at her. They seemed to ask, *What have you done with the real Maria Garcia?* and she followed up with, "Come! Let me show you the car. You'll love it! We'll take it for a drive and have lunch in Fuengirola."

She climbed behind the wheel and he got in the passenger side. "What's in Minsk?" he asked as the engine hummed impressively and they moved off.

"*Joder, Pepe!*" she said—which translates exactly to, "Fuck, Pepe!" but in tone and quality is more like, "Jesus, Pepe!" because the Spanish curse and swear copiously and fluently from an early age, and think nothing of it—"It's known for...um...abundant Soviet-era architecture, the Bolshoi Ballet Theatre, odd things like a Cat Museum, whose director is called Donut the Cat. Also there are primeval forests, incredible landscapes, the food is great..."

"A cat museum."

"Yes, darling."

"And the director is a cat—"

"Yes, darling, a cat called Donut. You'll love it. You'll see. We'll drive."

He was staring out of the window, shaking his head. Eventually he turned to face her. They were speeding along the highway, far above the glistening Mediterranean, racing past Benalmadena, with its Buddhist Stupa and the Butterfly Museum, but he saw none of that.

"What has happened to you, *cariño*? Are you in love? Is there somebody else? Are you having a midlife crisis? Is it a premature menopause? Tell me. We'll discuss it and get through it together. But please, stop this madness."

She laughed out loud and smacked his knee. "Don't be so *tonto*, José! We could use a holiday! Go somewhere different! See something different! Try new food, stay in a nice hotel. It will be wonderful, you'll see. And it won't cost us a penny!"

He didn't say anything to his wife. He just stared at her as she sped down the highway, weaving from lane to lane, overtaking the other, slower cars. He had never known his wife to drive so fast before. It was all part of that strange and unsettling day.

They went to La Carihuela on the seafront, and ate outside on the terrace. He ordered a small beer and she ordered glass of cold white wine, and while the waiter went to get their drinks she leaned across the table and covered his hand with hers.

"You know what I have been wanting for a long time?"

"What?" he asked her, with an unhappy feeling of dread in his belly as images of babies, dirty nappies and sleepless nights loomed in his imagination.

"A paella!"

He sighed with relief and breathed more easily. "Yes! Yes, paella. We should do that. We'll tell Emilio and Rosario to join us, and Juan and Rosa. We'll go to the *chiringuito* on the beach, one Sunday, maybe in July..."

He trailed off because she was smiling and shaking her head. "Now. I want it *now!*"

He narrowed his eyes, spread his hands, shrugged. It was a very Mediterranean gesture. "You have to order in advance. You know that. You order Friday or Saturday for Sunday. It takes a couple of hours to make..."

He trailed off because she was shaking her head again.

"I ordered it this morning from the office."

"You knew. You knew then that we were coming."

"I've known since April."

"You've booked the hotel in Minsk, too, haven't you?" She nodded and sipped. "How much did you win on the lottery, Maria? Maybe you should have told me, you know?"

"Sixty." He looked down at his cutlery and spent some time adjusting and straightening it. "Sixty thousand euros." He nodded, shrugged, looked up at her and nodded again. "You know, maybe you should have—it's a lot of money. Maybe you should have told...told..."

"What for? This is what I wanted to spend the money

on, José, and I am giving you the opportunity to enjoy it with me. Don't be ungrateful. Relax and enjoy it."

His mouth pinched into a prim beak. He reached for his beer and sipped it, leaving only the tiniest trace of foam on his upper lip.

"You seem different," he said. She picked up an olive and put it in her mouth, chewed watching him but said nothing. "When are we going, then? I'll have to pack. And we'll have to tell Emilio and Rosario, and Juan and Rosa. They're going to think you've gone crazy."

"*Cariño*," she dropped the olive stone in the saucer, "sometimes people go a little bit crazy. It's part of being normal." She gave a small laugh. "It's how we know we *are* normal, because we are doing something exceptional. You're forty, I'm thirty-five, and what have we ever done that was crazy or wild or exciting?"

He shrugged. "I have never done anything crazy or wild or exciting. Why would I? You, I don't know. You never tell me about your past. I always thought you were like me. But today, all of this..." He shook his head.

She sighed, aware she was taking the wrong tack with him. She reached across the table for his hand.

"We've been married five years, José. And for me they have been five very happy years. You have given my life stability." She nodded and after a moment repeated, "Stability. But just this once, *cariño*, just once, I would like to go on this little adventure. I am paying for everything with my money. We are perfectly safe, everything is as it should be. We just get in the car, drive across Europe, visit Minsk and come home. It will make me very, very happy. It will be something to tell our grandchildren about, if we ever get crazy enough to have children."

Nothing perceptible happened on her face. The smile was there, all her facial muscles were in the same place, but somehow the eyes went hard and cold, and all the warmth evaporated from her expression.

"You love me, don't you, José?" Her voice had become flat and mechanical. "You don't want to make me unhappy, do you?"

"No."

"I would be *very* unhappy if we didn't go tomorrow."

"No, no, that's not what I..."

The warmth flooded back and she squeezed his hand. "It would make me *so* happy. It would mean so much to me. You are such a good, supportive husband. You are my rock, *cariño*."

"It's just so sudden. So unexpected..."

She lifted his hand with both of hers and kissed it. "*Cariño*," she said, "it will be wonderful, we'll go via Barcelona, France, Switzerland, Germany, the Czech Republic, Poland and finally, Belarus—"

"*Dios mío!* How far is that?"

"Three thousand one hundred and thirty kilometers.[1]"

"More than *three thousand kilometers?*"

For a moment it seemed to him that her eyes lost all their humanity. If asked to put the feeling into words he would not have been able to, but it was as though, in her eyes, he saw her capacity for empathy shut down, as though the fuse had been removed, and her humanity had died.

"Six thousand kilometers there and back, my love, and I need you there by my side, happy and enjoying the adventure. Because if you don't, I will have to kill you and take somebody else."

They stared at each other for a long count of five, then her face creased and she burst out laughing. For a moment he did not laugh with her, but after a second his gape turned into a smile, and through sheer relief he too began to laugh.

"You had me worried!"

She nodded, still laughing. "Good!"

The paella arrived and was placed in the center of the table. José ordered another beer and rose to go to the bathroom. While she was alone Maria pulled her cell from her bag and called a number she had listed as "travel agents." It rang once and was answered immediately by a woman with a voice like sandpaper.

"Yes?"

"I think we are OK. He is very shocked, but I think he will adjust."

"Is he going to start talking to all his friends about your strange behavior? We cannot have that."

"I know, Colonel, but he will be with me at every moment. We will depart early tomorrow—"

"At what time?"

"Six AM. And he will see no one before that."

"Is it necessary to eliminate him and replace him?"

"No. It is safer this way. Perhaps on the return."

"Good. Keep me informed. There can be no mistakes, Maria."

"I know, Colonel. There will be no mistakes."

José came back from the bathroom and as he sat down she gazed at him with fond eyes and sighed, *"Ay, mi Pepe!"* She reached for his hand as he tried to pick up his fork, and turned that into a joke so that they both laughed. Then she started reminiscing about how they had met, and all the funny things that had happened to them up to the time they got married. Before long he was joining in, talking about how amazing it was that they had both passed their civil service exams with flying colors and both managed to land jobs in City Hall in Malaga.

"I never thought it could happen," he said. "I thought I'd get a moderately good pass. But you, you were so sure, so confident, as though you *knew.*"

"I did," she said simply. "It had to be. We had to be together. It was destiny." That, she thought, and the fact that the Russian Mafia owned City Hall in Malaga.

A couple of hours later she made him drive the Audi back home, telling him he had to get used to the car. She praised him at every opportunity, as though she were a little drunk, though she had had only half a glass of wine, and when they got home she dragged him to the bedroom and blew his mind.

While he slept she packed their cases and put their travel documents into her bag. Then she sat on the balcony with a gin and tonic and watched the sun set fire to the western horizon. On clear days like this you could see the black silhouettes of the Atlas Mountains in Africa, rising above the blood-red horizon. Africa and Europe, she thought, dead and dying empires. Soon the world would see a new empire, the greatest empire in history, and all others, the Chinese, the Europeans, the British and especially the Americans, would bow down before them.

The long winter of the Cold War was over, the great Bear was stirring, waking from hibernation. She smiled at the metaphor. It pleased her. Soon the Russian Bear would wake and roar. And, she thought, what would set it aside from all other empires was not its military might, though it was mighty indeed. No, it was its willingness to *use* that might, to visit hell and devastation on its enemies, without flinching. That was what set Russia aside from its enemies.

The hibernation was over, the Bear was awake.

ONE

AT ABOUT THE TIME THAT MARIA AND JOSÉ WERE crossing the Rhine from Altstadt in Switzerland to Konstanz in Germany, I was getting bored and drunk in Miami. I'd had about as much beach and pool as a man can take, and I was sitting in Jack Dusty's at the Ritz-Carlton in Sarasota. I was sipping my fourth martini and contemplating the word, "pinguid." It was a good word. It meant fatty, oily, greasy, unctuous. There was a guy sitting a couple of tables away talking to a high-class hooker who had brought the word into my mind. And that got me to thinking about taking early retirement, growing a beard and settling somewhere where I could write my memoirs, and use words like "pinguid." I figured I'd be the kind of writer who used a lot of alliteration. I'd create characters like Pinguid Pete, the greasiest don in Jersey, or Odontos Osmanek, the Cannibal of Constantinople.

I drained my glass, considered its emptiness for a moment, and wondered what Gallin was doing at that moment. The thought of Gallin made me decide I should probably not have another. I raised my hand to call the waiter and order a refill, when my cell rang. It was the distinctive ring of the office, so I sighed and pulled my phone from my pocket. Lovelock's voice oozed like pinguid hot chocolate in my ear.

"Hi sweetheart, Nero wants you to see the news, right now. Then get your skinny white ass to Bradenton Airport. There will be a plane waiting for you."

"If I do, will you dine with me tonight, Lovelock?"

"Sure I will, Mason. You just close your eyes and think of me. It'll be just like I was there, in the flesh..."

I sighed and went up to my suite. There I switched to the news channel, and sobered up fast. Kate O'Connor was standing outside the White House talking into the camera.

"...Jim, the word from the White House is that this is a hoax. A source very close to the president told me, in no uncertain terms, that this was, and I quote, 'bovine excrement.' But the rumors on social media persist. And so far all the major newspapers and broadcasters have received identical information, from a source identifying itself as the Russian Executive for the Dissemination of Sovietism—"

Jim's voice cut in and asked, "Kate, let me just stop you there for a moment, but the acronym for this name would be of course REDS. REDS, Soviets, these are terms we have not heard since the Cold War..."

"Yes, and that's partly why the White House and the Pentagon are being pretty dismissive of it. However, what Republican spokesman Mitch Bannon said to me, just a few minutes ago, was that Moscow has been showing ever stronger Soviet leanings in recent years, and that there are many in the Kremlin who favor a return to a more Soviet style of government. And he has a point, Jim. You just need to look at the recent invasion of Ukraine. The word among Republicans, and among the more hawkish Democrats, is that it would be a mistake to dismiss the claims of the REDS out of hand."

Jim's voice came back. "Kate, does this so-called Russian Executive claim to be connected in any way to the Kremlin or the Russian Government?"

"No such claim has been made, Jim. Neither has it been denied. From what I understand—and I stress this has *not* been confirmed—the president has telephoned Mr. Putin personally and demanded an explanation. Mr. Putin has categorically denied that the REDS organization has anything to do with them. It is, according to the Kremlin, a minor terrorist organization that by no stretch of the imagination has the resources to back up its claims."

"Kate, on the subject of those claims. Now, we are getting mixed, garbled messages, mainly from social media, about what the REDS claim to have done, or claim to be doing—can you shed any light on that?"

"Yes, Jim. We have an official statement from the Pentagon. It confirms that the Russian Executive for the Dissemination of Sovietism claims to have placed, or are in the process of placing, six TNDs—"

"TNDs, Kate, tell us what those are."

"TNDs, Jim, are tactical nuclear devices. Not to be confused with tactical nuclear weapons or warheads. The TND is essentially a small, portable nuclear bomb in a suitcase or a rucksack. It was first developed by the United States as far back as the late 1950s, when it was known as the W54.

"There have been major concerns about the existence and whereabouts of Soviet TNDs since the collapse of the Soviet Union, Jim, and it seems on May 30th, 1997 a congressional delegation met with General Aleksandr Lebed, the former Secretary of the Russian Security Council. During that meeting, General Lebed told the delegation he was aware that at least eighty-four of these portable nuclear devices had gone missing."

"That is extremely worrying."

"Yes, Jim, and in September of that same year, Lebed went on to state in interviews with CBS and *Sixty Minutes*, that the Russian military had lost more than a hundred out of a total of 250 'suitcase nuclear bombs.' He said specifically in those interviews that the devices were designed to look exactly like suitcases. So, Jim, we know that the devices exist, and we know that at least a hundred of them went missing amid the chaos of the collapse of the Soviet Union, over twenty years ago."

"That is pretty terrifying news, Kate. And now the REDS are claiming they have planted or are planting..."

"Six, at various locations around the United States. But here is the weird twist, Jim. They claim that five of the six are dummies, and only one is real, with the capacity to take out an entire medium-sized city. But, the discovery of any one of them, or the attempt to deactivate any one of them, *might* trigger the real bomb..."

I switched off the TV, had a strong, black coffee and packed my bags.

WHEN WE TOUCHED down at Ronald Reagan Airport there was a limo waiting which took me straight to the Commonwealth Tower on Wilson Boulevard. Ten minutes later I was admitted to Office 1I in what we fondly called Valhalla, Nero's inner sanctum. As the door closed behind me I sat in the chair across from him. He regarded me with eyes which were set in a face that was distinctly pinguid, but held all the menace of an impending storm.

"Well?" he said.

"The White House says it's bovine excrement. Is it?"

"It is neither bovine excrement nor equine excrement. And there will be no cover to be had anywhere if it hits the fan," he replied, stretching the metaphor to the breaking point. "Facts!" he snapped. "The Russian Executive for the Dissemination of Sovietism has contacted not only the social and news media, they have also directly contacted the CIA, the FBI, Military Intelligence at the Pentagon and the president at the White House. They assert that tactical nuclear devices capable of destroying a medium-sized city have been placed, or are being placed, at six locations..." He trailed off and arched an eyebrow because I was shaking my head. "No?" he asked.

"What is that," I said, "'have been placed, or are being placed'? What does that mean? They've been placed or they haven't."

"This whole enterprise, Alex, is about unsettling and unnerving, and attempting to provoke a state of chaos. The stock market crash of '29 did more damage to this country than either of the World Wars or the Cold War, and that was triggered by uncertainty and chaos. So, to engender that uncertainty and chaos they tell us that the devices have been placed, or are in the process of being placed. They will not tell us which. Equally, they do not tell us *where* they have been placed, or which is the authentic one."

"OK, I get that. They want to create an environment of uncertainty. But wouldn't it have been more effective, if they have a hundred of these damned suitcase devices, to plant six actual, real bombs?"

"No, Alex, because if six nuclear devices were detonated in the United States, then the country would be largely uninhabitable. And that is in nobody's interest. Also, if it is a risk to bring one nuclear device into the country, that risk is exponentially greater if you multiply it by six, because each discovery upon crossing customs increases the possibility that the other five will also be found. This way, five dummies can be made *in situ*, while only one need be smuggled in. And the uncertainty across the country caused by the fear of that single nuclear device, as it escalates toward fever pitch, will cause maximum economic damage while causing minimal logistical damage."

"That is subtle to the point of being fiendish."

"Fiendish." He nodded. "Indeed."

"And, from what I hear, finding and defusing them, whether they are dummies or not, could detonate the genuine one."

"That is what they have told us. Whether it is true or not, or some variation of the truth, we cannot know." He slipped a piece of paper across the desk. "They have given us these locations." I picked up the paper and read it aloud.

"Texas, New Mexico, Los Angeles, Washington DC, Silicon Valley and New York." I studied them a moment while Nero studied me. Finally I said, "Logic dictates that we should ignore this list on the basis that why the hell would they tell us where they were putting their bomb?" I shook my head. "But it's a double bluff. These locations make perfect sense. Texas: the oil fields. New Mexico: the Groom Lake facility and our most advanced military technology. Los Angeles: Hollywood: a major source of revenue, and our major propaganda machine. Washington DC: obviously because they would knock out our government and military HQ. Silicon Valley because it's Silicon Valley and some of the most advanced AI and IT research on the planet is there, and New York because it is the economic driver of the nation. They all make perfect sense as major targets."

"I agree."

"And if my purpose were to cripple the country politically and economically—"

"Alex," he raised a hand, "work it the other way. A process of elimination. Tell me what you would *not* do."

I frowned and scratched my ear. "OK, I would *not* nuke Texas. Because when the economy collapses I want to buy Texas, or at least its oil wells and its beef. The same logic applies to California as a whole and Silicon Valley in particular. There is technology there I would want for me. Again, the same applies to New Mexico. If they aim to destroy our economy, it's so they can move in, buy into our infrastructure and take possession of our technology and our resources."

"Good. So...?"

"So the two that stand out then as targets are Washington and New York. One for the political damage it will cause and the other for the economic damage."

He was nodding. "Exactly, but if you take out DC it is as

though you had dropped a bomb on New York at the same time. The collateral damage to the stock exchange would sink the economy overnight. Every major investor in the world would sell like crazy and pull his money out of the USA within hours. Within a day the country would be virtually bankrupted."

"So you think DC is the target? Isn't it too obvious?"

"Another double bluff. We are guaranteed to think it is too obvious and turn to New York or Texas as the more subtle targets. But Washington is the big prize, and let's face it, it is the one place where the actual physical, logistical damage is least. In fact some of the collateral damage is useful to them. The FBI on E Street, Norfolk, Arlington, us. We would all suffer terminal damage. Our capacity to govern, our capacity to defend ourselves and the national economy, would simply fold overnight."

"And Russia, in a show of brotherhood steps in to help us out, by buying up all our infrastructure, our resources and our military technology. And, declaring war on terrorism, imposes martial law."

"Something like that, yes."

"That's pretty far-out. It can't be that easy."

"Do you know how many suitcases enter the United States every year?"

"I can't say—"

He didn't let me finish. "Approximately one hundred and sixty million. Perhaps substantially more."

I nodded. "Fine, but those which are lined with lead are easily detected, as are those that are radioactive."

"Don't be facetious, Alex. I tell you constantly. A good proportion of those cases do not enter by plane, but by boat or across our northern and southern borders in the trunks of cars or RVs. A device shipped to Mexico in a crate labeled 'Machine Parts' and then brought across the border in the back of an RV driven by a happy, perfectly normal, un-pierced, un-tattooed family devoid of large black beards and *capitis* dishcloths, would go completely undetected. As you well know."

"It's a needle in a haystack. Where do you start?"

"Precisely. That is the genius of the thing."

"I mean, we don't even know what we're looking for."

Nero held up two fat fingers. "We are looking for two things. One, a suitcase or a rucksack which is out of place and has been there too long."

"OK, but that's one for the cops and security firms."

"Two, signs that a bomb has been assembled or placed somewhere."

I nodded. "OK," I nodded some more, thinking, "and signs that loose ends have been or are being tidied up."

"Good, you are thinking of homicides."

"Because an operation like this is going to require too many people. If they just brought the real bomb in and deto-nated it that could be almost untraceable. But they don't want that. They want to subject society and the economy to a prolonged period of stress and fear, right?"

"Correct."

"So they are going to need, in addition to the team who bring in the suitcase with the real device, maybe ten or twelve more people to put together and place the dummies. That is a big operation. Each one of those people is a poten-tial loose end. My guess is they are going to be eliminating those loose ends just as soon as they have done their jobs. So that is somewhere to start. Unexplained murders, in any of our six locations, which occurred within the last week or ten days."

He pressed a button on his desk. Lovejoy's exquisite voice said, "Yes, sir?"

"I want a list of all unexplained murders in the last week in Maryland, Virginia and DC, New York City, the Silicon Valley area, Los Angeles, Texas and New Mexico. Alert the state police and the FBI, we are looking for murders of people who have hitherto been more or less anonymous, and whose murder is apparently without motive. Have you got that?"

"Yes sir."

We went silent for a moment. I tried to wrack my brain for any other sign we might look for. I said, "Obviously customs and shipping companies are on high alert, airlines, airport security..."

"Yes, all the standard stuff has been seen to." He hesitated a moment, then said, "Of course, my theory about DC may be completely wrong. The fact is that any of those targets will have a very similar effect. We cannot focus on any one of them. The plan is brilliant."

I nodded. "I know." I made to stand. "Sir, is there anything else I need to know?"

He shook his head. "No, I'll be in touch if anything turns up."

"I'm going to check with contacts and sources."

"Every little bit helps."

Out on the sidewalk I looked for a cab. The nocturnal city glowed amber, and drowned out the stars. For a moment I was assaulted by the nightmare vision of DC as a wrecked, blackened graveyard of twisted steel girders and crumbling concrete. It had happened to Nagasaki and to Hiroshima. People, normal families, couples, children, had been going about their daily lives. A plane had appeared far above them, in the sky; most of them hadn't even seen it. Its payload dropped from its belly while the children played and people chatted, and it never even reached the ground.

The transition from "normal everyday" to total annihilation had happened in fractions of a second.

TWO

Twenty-six hours before that, Art Bernstein had sat in his car in the PMI Parking on H Street NW. He had left his two suitcases in his room at the Hotel Washington. Then he had gone out, explaining unnecessarily to the concierge that he was going out to a restaurant to dine.

As he'd climbed into his car and pressed the starter, his hands had been shaking. He'd cursed himself for making the concierge aware of him, but he seemed to have no control over his thoughts or his actions. He'd driven the short distance to the parking garage, and then sat there, trembling behind the wheel for five minutes. A voice in his head told him the attendant would notice if he didn't leave soon. So he took several deep breaths, then climbed out and made his way up in the elevator to the exit. His heart was racing and he could feel sweat trickling down his back. The attendant glanced up at him as he crossed the barrier and Art laughed and pointed to his breast pocket.

"Just checking my messages!"

The man didn't react. He just watched him leave and turned back to his TV or his magazine or whatever it was.

Art walked west to 14th Street and then turned south, according to the instructions he had been given. He had a barely controllable urge to weep like a child, and a humiliating desire to be with his mother. In his head he could still hear her voice in his head, nagging him that he had got it wrong again, like always, if it was possible to screw something up, trust Art to find the way. With his stupid, anxious nerves he had managed to get noticed by just about everyone he was meant to avoid.

If anybody asked him the attendant would say, "Yeah, oh yeah, there was this weird, grinning, sweating guy, tried to tell me about his telephone messages." And hadn't Anne told him that was the one thing to be really careful of?

"The thing everybody does, honey," she had said, "is to give too much unnecessary information. What you're doing, where you're going, why you are there, is nobody's goddamned business. OK?"

OK, she'd told him and he'd understood. But even so he was sweating like a horse, on the verge of tears and explaining to half of DC exactly why and what and who and where!

He came to the Ocean Prime on 14th Street and pushed through the door. A waiter approached him and he stammered. He said, "I..." four times while the waiter waited patiently, smiling kindly. Finally he managed, "...have a table reserved for two, Bernstein. There'll be two of us. A woman, lady, she'll be coming. I'm, I'm Bernstein..."

He stopped, telling himself it was too much information, and was none of the waiter's "goddamned business."

The waiter led him to a table for two, sat him down and asked if he would like a drink while he looked at the menu.

"Whiskey," he said, then blurted, "I don't normally drink whiskey, but today..."

He trailed off. The waiter smiled. "A special occasion. Any special whiskey?"

"Oh, um, scotch," and then again, "scotch. On the rocks."

He tried to read the menu but felt sick and faint at the thought of food. The whisky, when it came, seemed to settle his nerves a little, though.

After fifteen minutes the door opened and Anne came in. He saw her smile easily at the waiter, hand him her coat and point to Ash. He watched her cross the room and look down at him, smiling. They stayed like that a moment, she smiling at him, he staring at her, until she said, "Stand up, Art, and give me a kiss."

He almost tipped over his chair in doing so, then sat before she did and tried to stand again and almost overturned his glass. They finally settled themselves and Anne continued to smile at him. Her eyes, a dark, settling blue, seemed kind and compassionate. Her lips, small but full, were very kissable. He closed his eyes and heard his breath shake as he sighed.

"I'm having..." He paused to get his breath under control. "I'm having a really hard time."

She gave a small laugh that was not unkind. "I can see that."

He reached for his glass. "In fact, I seem to be going to pieces. I'm afraid you chose the wrong guy. I'm not cut out for this."

Her expression didn't change, but she said, "Shut up, Art."

He closed his eyes and nodded, then said, "See what I mean?"

She leaned across the table, still smiling, and reached for his hand.

"Art, let me put your mind at rest on a couple of issues."

She sat back, but didn't take her eyes off him or stop smiling, as the waiter placed a tall gin and tonic in front of her. When he'd gone she leaned forward and took his hand again. He felt a strange warmth in his belly.

"First," she said. "It's been called off, so you are off the hook."

A rush of relief flooded through him so that he almost peed in his pants. "Oh, God," he said. She smiled on one side of her face and half whispered, "Keep it under control, Art."

"Yes, yes, but oh God, oh God, thank you!"

"Second, I don't know if you realize the kind of stress you've been under these past few days."

"What?"

She picked up the menu and gazed at it a moment with an arched eyebrow, then signaled the waiter. He came over and she told him, "We'll share a dozen oyster and a bottle of Dom, very cold, and then we'll have a couple of sirloin steaks, medium rare, salad no fries. And we'll have a Pomerol, open it now so it can breathe for a bit." She spread her hands and pulled down her mouth, thinking. "A Chateau Gazin? Twenty fifteen, sixteen, seventeen? They were all good years."

The waiter bowed and went away.

Art gave a small, nervous laugh. "Wow," he said. "You

know all that stuff. I'm out with a girl who... I mean, you're like a female version of James Bond, right? S...s...s...," he said it five times in all before he finally came out with, "...sexy too."

"Thank you." She shook her head. "I have to tell you, I think it's incredible."

"What is?"

He watched her sip her drink, then lick her lips with a very pink tongue.

"You." She said it without looking at him.

"Me. I'm incredible?"

"I work with all sorts of people, Art. SEALs, Special Forces, CIA—we call CIA officers Company Men. People who are accustomed to operating under a lot of pressure. But let me tell you something, Art. They always have backup. They always have a safety net, somebody they can turn to for support. But in the last week you have borne this whole thing completely on your own, without support, knowing what was at stake at every moment, and yet you saw it through. You stayed with it and you did not waver."

She let her eyes rove over his face and his chest and smiled. "OK, so you're not built like Schwarzenegger, you're not trained to kill like James Bond, but you have more sheer steel in you than both of them put together."

His face flushed. "Are you serious?"

"I am, very, and I have to tell you I find it very attractive."

"You're kidding." She shook her head. "You're not kidding."

"You have no training, no background, nothing. But you stepped up like a man. Inside, you thought you were going to screw up at any moment. But did you run? Did you go to pieces?"

"No."

"No, and I find that much more admirable, and..." She allowed a slow smile to curl her lips. "...and sexy, than all the muscles and training in the world."

The waiters brought the oysters and the champagne.

From that point on Art entered a kind of heavenly dream state. This was the woman who had threatened to torture and kill his mother, his brother, his brother's wife and their two small children. This was the woman who had blackmailed him into risking his life to commit a crime, a crime which could have landed him in prison for the rest of his life, without ever knowing what the crime was. And yet, there she sat, opposite him, with her blonde curls, her pretty lips and her kind blue eyes; her long earrings sparkling beside her long, smooth neck, telling him she found him attractive and sexy. And he, his bloodstream and his brain flooded with dopamine, was falling in love with her. It was nuts, but it was happening, right there in that fancy restaurant, eating oysters and drinking French champagne.

They took away the empty bottle and the oyster shells and brought the Claret and the steak. At some point he'd smiled at her from under his eyebrows and told her, "You know, if your people wanted to train me, I'd be available for that..."

She had looked interested and said, "OK, good to know. I'll talk to them upstairs."

He'd leaned back and laughed softly, holding his wine. "Given appropriate remuneration, obviously."

She had leaned forward. "Oh, honey, they know how to pay, believe me."

He had paid with his credit card and she had assured him it would be put down to expenses, along with the hotel, the gas, and anything else he wanted to claim. Then outside, she had grabbed his lapels and whispered, "Did you leave the car where I told you?"

"Yes, of course."

"We can't go to your room in the hotel, it would attract too much attention, but we can go to the car."

They had walked fast. It was just two blocks. She had told him to go in first and get in behind the wheel, and she had followed thirty seconds later, hunched over with her scarf over her face. She had got in next to him, grabbed his head with her left hand and snarled, "Kiss me hard!"

He had grabbed her face with both hands and pressed his lips to hers, just as she rammed the seven-inch, razor-sharp blade between his ribs. It was not a broad blade, no more than a quarter of an inch at the base, but it was long and sharp enough to cut a single hair in freefall. She drove it home all the way, though his heart and to the back of his ribcage. For a few seconds he struggled and thrashed, but she gripped him tight, holding her mouth to his, feeling the thrill of his ebbing life, imagining in her private fantasy that she was sucking his life into her own body, to make her stronger.

Then he sagged and went limp, and she let him go. She whispered in his ear, "So much better than sex, Art. Thank you."

She withdrew the blade and wiped it clean on his shirt, then slipped it back in her bag. After that she made her way to her own car one floor up, avoiding the security cameras, and left the parking garage to disappear into the dark, amber Washington night.

Three hours later, having abandoned the car and wiped all her prints from it, she took a taxi to the Ronald Reagan International Airport and boarded a flight to Los Angeles, with just half an hour to spare before take-off. Fortunately she had already checked in to business class as Elena Antyukh, and had only hand baggage. She made the plane with fifteen minutes to spare and, as they soared high over the blackness of West Virginia, she called the stewardess and ordered a large gin and tonic.

Art's body was found early in the morning, when Ben came on duty. His name was Antonio Bennini, but everybody called him Ben. Other guys at the garage were not really interested. They read their magazines or watched the TV, but Ben liked to do things right. And he noticed, when he was reviewing the cameras, that there was something reflecting the light in the driver's seat of Art's Honda. When he looked again half an hour later it was still there. So at seven thirty he made his way down to the third basement and approached the car, shining his flashlight in through the windshield. The expression on Art's face almost made him fall over. He ran back to the office and immediately called the cops.

"It's like he died of fright," he told them when they got there. "There's no blood, no wounds, nothin'. But man, his face! His teeth bared, his eyes wide open like saucers—man!"

It took Sergeant Greene and his partner about three minutes to find the exquisite wound. At first it just looked like a small tear in his shirt. But when Sergeant Greene had noticed the vest underneath was damp and stained with a small amount of blood, he had explored further and realized it was a very odd homicide. He had called dispatch and within twenty minutes the garage was sealed off and the scene of crime officers were swarming all over the car and the security cameras like ants.

Later, at the morgue, the ME had told Detective Woods, over Art's bare, dead chest, "In my thirty years as a medical practitioner I have never actually seen one of these till now."

Detective Woods, who had seen most things at least once, said, "One of what?"

"A stiletto wound," he said, peering at it and probing it with latex fingers. "I have read about them, obviously. It was a very popular form of assassination in Renaissance Italy. But I have never actually seen one before. Beautifully done. Very clean, very precise. I'd say your killer has certainly done this before. It penetrated effortlessly right between the ribs, through the heart, and actually reached the back of the ribcage. It paralyzed the heart in the process and caused minimal bleeding."

"So he was stabbed in the heart with a razor-sharp stiletto while he was sitting behind the wheel of his car, in a parking garage?"

"Yes, but he was turned slightly to his right. He had lipstick smeared on his mouth and on his ear, and fine, blonde hairs gripped in his fingers."

"Sweet Jesus! You want to explain to me..." He trailed off, shifting his weight from one foot to another. "I mean, what? Art Bernstein, accountant from Annapolis, never married, lives with his mother, no priors, winds up stabbed through the heart with a stiletto, by a pro, while she kissed him in the front seat of his car? Is that it? Is that what you're telling me? What, aside from everything, is wrong with that picture?"

The ME shrugged. "You're the detective. You interpret. I simply give you the facts. And here's another couple of facts to screw with your brain."

"More?"

The ME nodded and giggled. "His last supper, so to speak, was oysters, a very good sirloin steak, champagne and red wine."

The door opened and Chavez, Woods' partner, came in holding his cell. He drew breath but Woods held up his hand. "Wait—"

"What I miss?"

"Who is this guy? James Bond? You're telling me he has dinner with a blonde wearing lipstick, they do the whole thing, oysters, champagne, a fine steak and fine wine. Then, they don't go to his hotel or her hotel, they go to the parking garage to make out, and while she's kissing him she stabs him, expertly, in the heart with a stiletto. That is the stupidest story I ever heard." He stared hard at Chavez, who stared back. "And there's more. Not only is this dame a pro, she casually leaves behind her lipstick all over his face, plus her saliva and her hair. Why didn't she just leave her social security number written on his dick in eyebrow pencil?" He turned to the ME like it was his fault it didn't make sense. "She didn't, did she?"

"I'll send you the report in the morning."

Greene turned to Chavez and said, "What?" referring incongruously to the call he had received five minutes earlier.

"First, while I think of it, if he parked on H Street and brought the dame back to his car, means they ate nearby."

"Obviously."

"Steak and oysters near PMI Parking on H Street NW gotta be Ocean Prime on 14th. Two blocks away."

"No shit, Sherlock. What was the call?"

"The chief. If we come across any unusual homicides, we should call this number at the Pentagon."

"The Secret Service?"

"That's what I thought at first, but it ain't the usual liaison number."

"Oh, that's great. That's just superb!"

THREE

THE SECOND DISTRICT HAD ITS STATIONHOUSE ON Idaho Avenue, in the leafy suburbs of Cleveland Park, some three or four miles from the White House. It was an ugly, concrete and glass box surrounded by what looked to my urban eye like pin oaks, but might have been almost anything else. They were trees and gave leafy shade, and that was where I parked my Factory Five Mk4 Roadster and made my way through the early morning sun to meet Detectives Greene and Chavez.

We met in a small conference room on the second floor, with large windows overlooking a parking lot and the Newark Community Gardens. Greene and Chavez were seated, unshaven, at a long, melamine table. They had heavy shadows under their eyes that said they blamed me for not having been able to sleep last night. Each had a brown manila envelope in front of him, and there was a third on my side of the table.

"Good morning." I nodded and reached across the table to shake their hands. "Alex Mason."

They told me their names and I sat.

"Let me say right from the start that this is not an invasion of your jurisdiction. We don't even know for sure that we are interested in this case—"

Greene cut in, "Who's 'we'?"

"Need to know, but just think of it as the federal government."

"So the Feds."

"Or the CIA, DEA, Military Intelligence, NSA, Secret Service... Any of those, take your pick. So why I am here is to satisfy myself that this homicide has nothing to do with a parallel investigation."

Chavez shrugged. "OK, so how can we help, Mr.—" He hesitated. "Mister, right? Not Agent, Officer, Captain?"

I smiled. "Keep fishing and we might recruit you. We admire tenacity. Mister will do fine. You can help me by giving me the details of the homicide, and any theories you may have developed, however speculative."

Greene grunted and then sighed heavily.

"Art Bernstein, forty years old, non-practicing Jew, father died of cancer when he was a kid, one younger brother married with two children. Art lived with his mother in Annapolis, address is in the file. He owned his house, ten grand left on his mortgage will be paid by his insurance. Leaves his mother a pension of three grand a month till she dies."

Chavez took over like they had rehearsed it.

"He worked as an accountant at Stevens and Wright, had no financial debts and he leaves savings and investments of around one hundred grand. From what we can ascertain so far, he had no enemies, no bad habits, didn't even go with women." He spread his hands and shrugged, looking down at his closed file. "Now, he shows up yesterday, parks his car in the PMI Parking Garage on H Street NW and walks down to 14th Street, two blocks, to Ocean Prime. The waiter says he had reserved a table for two, he was real nervous when he arrived and ordered a scotch. Said he never really drank but that night was somehow special."

"He said that?"

"Yeah."

Now Greene cut in again. "Fifteen minutes later a broad shows up. Late twenties, blonde, good-looking but not drop-dead gorgeous. They get cozy, she keeps holding his hand, and she orders the meal for them both: a dozen oysters, bottle of French champagne, then two sirloin steaks and a bottle of expensive French red wine."

Chavez said, "Yeah, she knew the wine she wanted." He flipped open his file and leafed through the papers. "Maybe it's nothing, you know? But it seemed odd to me, a dame knowing about wine like that. Pomerol." He glanced at me. "Is that a wine?"

I nodded. "It's a wine-producing area in Bordeaux."

"Right. So she wanted a Chateau Gazin, and it had to be twenty-fifteen, sixteen or seventeen. She was very specific about that."

Greene went on, "So they got affectionate during the meal and they left together. Next thing we know the parking attendant in the PMI calls to report a homicide. Antonio Bennini. His name's in the file. So Art is sitting behind the wheel of his car. He is turned slightly toward the passenger seat. He has an expression on his face like he's just seen the devil himself, and there's no immediate sign of a cause of death. Except, when I started snooping around I see his shirt is torn just over his heart, and when I look I see his vest, underneath, has a small amount of blood. Turns out he was stabbed with," he turned to Chavez and they both said it together, "a stiletto." They both nodded at me and Greene went on.

"A long, slim blade, about seven inches, with razor-sharp tip and edges. And get this, according to the ME, the killer was an expert and had made that kind of kill before."

Chavez cut in, leaning forward, "But the bit that freaks me? She's making out with the victim when she kills him. He has lipstick smeared all over his mouth, and he has strands of blonde hair gripped in his hands. So they are kissing, making out, and the bitch drives a knife through his heart. Is that a bitch or what? If that ain't a bitch I don't know what is."

"The lab is running DNA and the lipstick?"

"Sure."

"How about fingerprints?"

"They're going over the car as we speak."

I opened the file and went through the photographs and the ME's report. "The ME considers that the stabbing was done by an experienced professional," I looked up, "yet she is sloppy and careless about leaving behind DNA and finger-prints. Any thoughts?"

Greene shrugged. "I'm thinking what you're probably thinking. She knows she's not in AFIS or CODIS, and if she knows that it's either because she lives in a jurisdiction which does not have law enforcement agreements with the USA, or she lives here but has never worked here before."

I looked at Chavez. He shrugged. "We ain't got no hits so far. To me it's the only explanation that makes sense."

"Anything else? What about his bank and credit card? Did he book a hotel?"

"We only got the call a few hours ago, but so far neither his current account nor his credit card shows a charge for a hotel."

"So she booked it."

Chavez made a "not necessarily" face by pulling down the corners of his mouth. "He maybe drove in for the day. It's a half hour, forty-five minutes from Annapolis."

I smiled. "I might agree, if he hadn't reserved a table at Ocean Prime and had a dozen oysters, a bottle of champagne and a bottle of claret. On that kind of adventure, you make sure you have a bed waiting for you nearby."

He shrugged. "I guess."

I nodded. "She booked the hotel. I need you to—"

Greene's eyebrows rose high on his head. "Excuse me? *You* need us?"

"Yes, Detective Greene, and I apologize if this wasn't made clear to you. Until I decide this case is of no interest to us, it is under my jurisdiction. That means it is under federal jurisdiction, and when you talk to me, it's like you're talking to the president."

He sighed, looked away and muttered something at the window. I ignored him and went on.

"I need you to check all the hotels in the immediate vicinity of the Ocean Prime. Maybe he was booked in as Art Bernstein, maybe he wasn't. So you need to show them photographs. A guy who checked into his room, was maybe very nervous and acting odd, and never returned to his room. Any questions?"

They shook their heads. I gave them my card.

"Keep me in the loop and let me know of any developments. Particularly DNA and prints. I'd really like to know the identity of this woman."

Greene's face said he was unamused. "Yeah, so would we. If you've got anything that can help *us*..."

"All I've got, Detective Greene, is questions. I'm not sure yet this case is even relevant to our investigation. But if anything comes up I think you can use, I'll let you know."

"Yeah, right."

Chavez said, "We appreciate it."

I stood and gathered up the file they'd given me. Greene remained seated, watching me.

"What is this, terrorism? Islamic jihad or something? Suitcases...?"

I paused, thinking about it and looking at the silent, peaceful scene outside the window. Eventually I nodded and looked him in the eye. "Something," I said. "More something than Islamic jihad."

Outside I climbed into my car and sat squinting at the trees in the sun. Reckless but in control, experienced, professional, but the MO rang absolutely no bells. I fired up the big brute of an engine and growled slowly down Idaho Avenue toward Massachusetts Avenue, wondering whether it was worth driving over to Annapolis and talking to Mrs. Bernstein about her son. As I drove and thought I absently called Aila Gallin at the London Mossad office. I knew from her tone that she was pleased to hear from me.

"What?"

"Female, blonde, kills male victim while making out, by sliding a very sharp stiletto into his heart. Is careless about leaving DNA and fingerprints at crime scene in DC."

"Is this your suitcase problem?"

"Mm-hmm."

"Never heard of an MO like that. You sure she's a pro?"

"The ME thinks she's done it before."

"Who's your victim?"

I thought about it. "Nobody. A forty-year-old accountant who lived with his mother. No debts, no enemies, no priors. The MO is not familiar to you?"

"No, I'll ask around, but it isn't ringing any bells. Have you got a theory?"

"I have a bit of one. She seduces him or blackmails him, or both, into planting a suitcase. She chooses him because he is a nobody and nobody will ever suspect him of anything. She books him into a hotel, and after he has checked in and deposited his cases—one of them being the bomb—she arranges to meet him at a nearby restaurant. After dinner, she goes with him to his car and kills him."

"Why kill him? That's only going to draw attention to him."

"Attention is good. This whole suitcase business is about drawing attention. What she doesn't want is a loose end, or anyone who can tell us where the suitcase is."

"So she kills him to silence him after he has placed his suitcase, but in such a way to attract media attention."

I nodded at the abundant trees in their new spring green as I entered Observatory Circle.

"That's how it looks to me right now."

"Makes sense. I'm guessing you have eliminated the other obvious possibilities."

"There don't seem to be any other obvious possibilities. The important thing, the MO, it is not familiar to you?"

"Nope."

We exchanged farewells and I hung up. At Dupont Circle, still not exactly sure where I was going, my cell rang. It was Lovelock.

"Where are you, handsome?"

"A little lost around Dupont Circle."

"Well make your way back to mama, baby, I have plane tickets for you."

"For me? Why? Where am I going?"

"Y'all are goin' to Texas, baby, where everything is bigger and better."

"What for? Have I got time to—"

"Uh-uh, you got time to get yourself here, talk to the chief and get yourself out to the airport. You're on the next flight out of here."

"OK, I'm on my way."

I made a small detour around K Street and Constitution Avenue, counting how many hotels I could find in the immediate vicinity of the White House. I counted ten, just on a quick fly-by. I swore gently under my breath and accelerated away toward Virginia and ODIN HQ.

Nero was sitting at his desk when I arrived, looking sour.

"I suppose you'd better sit down," he said. "But don't get comfortable. You have very little time and we can't be forever providing you with private jets."

"No sir."

I sat.

"I don't know if you realize this, Alex, but it seems that practically all homicides are peculiar and unusual, at least to begin with."

"No, sir."

"And then when you look into them it turns out either A was jealous of B and therefore killed C, or B, or both B *and* C. Or that A wanted something that B had and killed B to get it."

"I see."

"There is currently a flood of these cases into ODIN and we have staff seconded from other jobs they should be doing in order to filter through these homicides looking for ones that might relate to our suitcase bombs."

"I am almost certain the PMI Parking Garage killing on H Street is relevant, sir, and I would like to start visiting the hotels..."

I trailed off because he was flapping his hand at me. "Very good, excellent, let the local MPD take care of it. I need you to go to Texas."

"What for, sir?"

"Because, Alex, there has been a murder there for which no satisfactory explanation is immediately apparent and I should like you, if you would be so kind, to go and investigate it, in the light of the suitcase bombs."

I stifled a sigh and stood. As I reached for the door handle I said quickly, "Female blonde kills male victim while making out in his car by sliding a very sharp stiletto into his heart, three hundred and fifty yards from the White House. She is unconcerned about leaving DNA and fingerprints at crime scene though ME says she kills like a pro. Victim is Art Bernstein, a forty-year-old accountant who lives with his mother. No debts, no enemies, no priors. Is the MO familiar to you?"

He was very still and very quiet. Finally he said, "No. There are a dozen hotels in that area."

"And I need to canvas them. There could be a nuclear device sitting in any one of them right now."

"No. I need you in Texas."

"Then, sir, please talk to the chief of the Metropolitan Police Department and tell him to order, directly, Detectives Greene and Chavez of the 2nd District to canvas each one of those hotels. The room was booked by her, not him, and we don't know in what name."

"Go away. Lovejoy will give you your ticket. Go to Texas."

I left his office and Lovejoy handed me a large manila envelope.

"Tickets, boarding pass, no time for luggage, buy whatever you need there on company expenses. You'll be met at Midland Airpark by Detective Seth Macdonald, the investigating officer. That gives you three hours to study the file."

I took the envelope. "Thanks. Keep me posted with any developments." I was about to open my mouth to add something witty, but she pointed to the door. "You have a taxi waiting downstairs."

Despite Nero's winging to the contrary, the plane was a company Gulfstream. I had no luggage, as Lovelock had observed, so I was slung on board, strapped in and provided with lunch and a couple of dry martinis as we soared southwest across the continent, and I made my way painstakingly through what little there was of the report.

FOUR

DETECTIVE SETH MACDONALD WAS TALL AND wore boots and a hat. He also had very white teeth which he displayed in a manly grin, and very blue eyes that told you not to worry, Texas would take care of everything. He shook my hand like he'd been waiting all his life to do it, slapped me on the shoulder and guided me toward a RAM 1500 TRX with a City of Midland Police badge on the door.

"I appreciate your coming over, Mr. Mason. We don't get many homicides here in a year."

He hauled open the door and climbed behind the wheel while I hauled myself in the passenger side. The big engine growled and rumbled, and we pulled out of the parking lot as he kept talking.

"Most years we maybe get one or two, in a bad year we might get three. But there ain't never no mystery about 'em. They're almost always the same." He grinned at me with his very white teeth and his eyes seemed to sparkle. "Either some boy thinks his wife or his girlfriend is seein' another man, or she *is* seein' another man. So he gits his gun and he kills the boy, or he kills the girl, or, in a bad year, he kills 'em both." He laughed. "When you have a population of a hundred and forty thousand people, it don't take much to push up the statistics of murders per hundred thousand inhabitants!"

I smiled. "I see what you mean."

"If he finds them both in the bed, chances are it's gonna be a bad year, statistically. But if he kills his man in the bar, when he's drunk, he'll probably have cooled off by the time he finds his woman."

"So that'll be a good year, statistically."

"See what I mean?"

We'd been cruising down North Big Spring Street while he enlightened me on the statistical impact of pillow talk and post-coital cigarettes with your illicit lover when being discovered by your spouse, but now we crossed over a small river and turned left onto Scharbauer Drive, past Bush's Chicken. I wondered if there was any connection between the chickens and the presidents who had hailed from this town. I didn't ask because Macdonald was still talking.

"But this killing has us foxed, Mr. Mason. We can't make head nor tail of it. For a start, the victim don't seem to be from Midland. Nobody knows him, so far nobody has reported him missing and nobody's come forward to identify him or claim him. And in the second place, ninety percent of killings that happen here—and like I'm tellin' you, we are below the national average *and* the Texas average —what killings happen here are almost always with a gun. This is gun territory. Hell, everybody's got a gun here. And if they don't shoot each other, then they beat each other to death with their fists."

"But that wasn't the case here."

"No sir."

We'd come off Scharbauer Drive and now we were moving sedately down Chukar Lane, among fertile fields, white picket fences and pleasant houses set among trees and well-tended fields. Next thing we crossed the I-20 and then the railway line and found ourselves in the broad, massive sprawl of the Texrange Oil and Gas Corporation. Here there were no white picket fences, and no pleasant, ordered country homes or fields. Here there was red and gray dust, huge cylindrical gas towers looming against the blue sky, massive pipelines which channeled oil and gas across a torn, broken landscape, and tankers, hundreds of tankers parked on vast patches of wasteland. Everything was steel and dry dirt. I saw no people.

We rolled through this landscape from Armageddon, trailing a huge plume of red and gray dust, and came finally to the intersection with East County Road 90. From there we turned through a gate to a small farm where we rolled and bumped and lurched our way through barns and sheds, down a narrow, muddy track to stop at the banks of a small river, shrouded on either side by dense trees.

I followed Detective Macdonald down the muddy bank to the edge of the water, where yellow tape had been strung from tree to tree, covering an area of about five hundred square yards. He lifted the tape for me and I ducked under.

I saw the spot before he pointed to it. It was an indentation in the soft mud beside the water, a little less than six feet long, about two feet at its widest point.

"That's where he was found?"

"Yup. Dogs from the farm found him. Started yelpin'

and howlin' till the kids came down." He smiled. "Thought maybe it was an alligator. They been findin' alligators in the Texas Colorado, and the kids thought maybe one had found its way here. Kids! But it weren't no alligator. It was a dead man."

"In the report it said there were tracks."

I was looking around but couldn't see them. He pointed upstream and I followed him for a few yards, where he stopped and pointed again across the stream. There I could see a scattered line of deep footprints.

"We made casts of the best ones. Looks like there were two individuals. One set of prints matched the victim, the other we assume was the killer. Looks like a big man, tall, size thirteen boots. Weird thing is, you can see them both arrive together. They hopped over the fence yonder by the road and come down along the far bank, then crossed through the water to the spot there, where he was killed. But you don't see no tracks where the killer left."

I gazed back toward the road. "He left along the river to the blacktop."

"That's what we figured," he shrugged, "but what for? We already got his boot prints from where he arrived! He comes tramping in like he don't give a damn. But when he leaves..." He shrugged and shook his head. "Don't make much sense."

I said, half to myself, "Because he wanted us to know he'd been here. He wanted us to know that his victim trusted him. He wasn't chasing him. They were walking together for some purpose. But once he'd killed him he didn't want us to know where he'd gone."

"Yeah..." He nodded. "That's about the only way to read it. Still don't make a whole lot a sense, though."

"They didn't hear anything in the farm?"

"No, not till the dogs started going crazy."

I had a snoop around but found nothing of any interest. "I guess the crime scene guys have been over the place pretty thoroughly, huh?"

"With a fine-toothed comb and a magnifying glass."

"OK, thanks. Let's go see the body."

It was a short drive to the ME on Main Street. He was a man in his sixties who, at a rate of two or three murders a year over a career spanning four decades, had grown accustomed to human tragedy and the stupid waste of human life that so often goes with it. As he led the way through the institutional fire doors he spoke without looking back at me.

"So what makes this one special?"

"That's what I am hoping you will tell me."

"That's a new one!" He laughed. "DC shuttin' its trap to see what Texas has to say."

He chuckled and I smiled. "I thought DC was run from Texas. This is oil we're standing on, right?"

He snorted and approached the refrigerated drawers. He pulled one out and drew back the white sheet to reveal a blond man in his mid twenties. His hair was long, below his shoulders, and he had a well-trimmed beard and moustache. He was tanned and athletic and had all the appearance of the stereotypic Californian beach boy.

"No surfboard?"

Macdonald snorted. "No nothin'. No papers, no ID, no hits on AFIS or CODIS. Just a dead man."

I bent over and examined his chest where a one-inch cut

could be seen just over the fifth intercostal. "And the report says that he was stabbed through the heart?"

The ME cleared his throat.

"That's the exit wound. You can tell because the skin forms a flap, torn from the inside out, and there is no bruising. Here, help me turn him over..."

Between the three of us we turned him on his front and the ME continued talking, pointing at a deep, bruised cut just beside his left shoulder blade.

"See here? The cut is wider, indicating a tapered blade. You can also see from the bruising that it was thrust in hard and driven all the way home, rupturing the small blood vessels when the hilt struck the skin. Whoever killed him was not only very skilled, but very strong."

I nodded. "The trajectory of the blade is absolutely straight. That takes a lot of practice and skill. But what kind of weapon are we talking about?" I frowned. "This is a blade of, what? At least twelve inches, more like fifteen, and a width of one and a half inches at the hilt."

The ME was nodding. "Yup, and double-edged."

"It's a sword. A short, double-edged sword, or a very long dagger."

"That would be consistent."

Detective Macdonald said, "You see why I told your chief it was an unusual homicide."

"I do see that, Detective Macdonald. I see that very clearly. Listen, I am going to have to talk to your chief, urgently, like an hour ago."

It was half a mile in a straight line up Maine Street, and les than ten minutes later I was shaking hands with Chief Hanratty as he stared at me with narrowed eyes that were trying to see inside my skull. I didn't give him time to ask what the hell it was all about. I started telling him before my ass hit the chair he was pointing at.

"This is about suitcase bombs," I said. "Nuclear ones."

Macdonald's jaw went slack, but Hanratty grunted. "I had a feeling," he said.

"We're flying by the seat of our pants and piecing this together as we go," I told him. "But what we seem to have so far is this: a victim is lured into taking a suitcase to a hotel. The victim does not book the room, the killer does, probably for several days. So even if you establish the identity of the victim, you can't use their financials to find out what hotel they're booked into. Once the suitcase is deposited in the room, the victim is killed, severing the loose end and making it very difficult to locate the suitcase."

"So in some hotel in Midland, there is one of those cases," said Hanratty. "It might be a dummy or it might be real. We got the Permian Basin, the Wasson Field, the Wolfberry Play and the Spraberry Trend, not to mention the |Bone Spring Formation and Yates Field. We're talking about an area of twenty to twenty-five thousand square miles which produces most of the oil in the United States of America. If this area is contaminated with radiation—leavin' aside all the folks who will die—the economy of this country will collapse."

I nodded. "That seems to be the plan. So I am going to need you to go to each and every hotel and check their registers for a man matching the deceased's description who booked in but never showed up again."

"I'm on it. Macdonald, start forming teams. Drop everything else and start getting teams out there! Now!"

Macdonald strode out and Chief Hanratty skewered me with his eyes again.

"Is it Texas? Is Texas the target?"

"We don't know, Chief. That's the whole point of the plan. The target is the American economy, but the bomb could be in any one of the six locations, or there could be more than one—or none. They want to screw with our heads and cause a crash in the stock market." I hesitated, reluctant to give false hope if I was wrong. "My guess, if it were me, I would want to keep the oil wells functional and usable. It's a priceless resource. If it were me I'd pick a place that would have maximum economic impact, but physically would be a minimal loss."

He gave a grim laugh. "Sounds like DC to me. No offense, like."

"None taken, I tend to agree."

I stood and he stood with me, then paused and shook his head. "Forgive my askin', Mr. Mason, but seems to me you just don't know which way the blows are comin'. I mean, there is three hundred and twenty-nine million people in this federation, and that many possible locations for your suitcase, multiplied by the number of places each of those people might have been in the last four or five days. I figure that gives you roughly a billion places that suitcase might be. Hell! You got us lookin' in hotel rooms, but it might just as easily be buried in the roots of any of the trees where John Doe was found!"

I let him finish and nodded. "You're right," I said. "But if I start thinking that way, I might as well take your Smith and Wesson and blow my brains out. We have to try and imagine which risks the Russians will be likely to take, and which they're likely to avoid. And, end of the day, an untraceable hotel room is a better bet than a riverbank. And a stranger in town suggests a hotel."

He gave his head a twitch. "I hope you're right, Mr. Mason. I sure hope you're right."

"So do I. If you find the room and a case, call me directly. We have our own specialists who will deal with it. We don't know if they are booby trapped, but the chances are they will be. So you seal off the area and you call us at this number. Do not under any circumstances move the case or try to open it."

He looked at the number. "Ten four. I'll let the boys know."

I got a cab back to the airport and, as we hurtled down the runway, lurched and soared into the great blue expanse of the sky, I called Nero.

"Speak!"

"Does two make a pattern?"

"Talk sense. What are you talking about?"

"Lured to a quiet place and stabbed in the heart with a fifteen-inch blade, possibly mediaeval. Careless about leaving tracks on arrival, careful to leave no tracks on departure, victim is a stranger in town. However, in this case there is no ID, no papers, no driver's permit. Nothing, we have no idea who he is."

"But we must assume he was used to deliver a suitcase to a hotel room."

"I'd say so. But sir, if this is the technique they are using, it gives us some idea of the timeframe we have."

"A dangerous assumption."

"The *maximum* timeframe we have. Because if they

don't return to their rooms within a week, and they can't contact the guest in question, there is a good chance they will open those cases."

"Yes, and in all probability detonate the bomb. Still, I think we knew we had less than a week anyway. What is your next move?"

"My next move, sir? Well, as soon as the stewardess can walk down the aisle without either holding on or falling over, I plan to ask her for a very dry martini."

FIVE

Meanwhile, in Texas, things were not quite as they seemed. Amongst other things, Jamil was sitting outside the Midland Memorial Hospital in the dark, hemorrhaging internally and urgently in need of a doctor. Semidelirious, he was trying to remember how things had got so badly out of hand. Things had not gone as planned.

He had booked Chet's room at the Holiday Inn on Crump Street, as instructed. He had met him at the Greyhound stop on Garden City Highway and driven him to the hotel, all as planned, all as ordered by the colonel. He had instructed Chet to go and check in and deposit the suitcase and the bag. Chet had been cool and done this as instructed. There had been no problem, everything had gone well.

Until he returned from checking in and had climbed in the car beside Jamil. As they had driven off he had started to ask questions, and Jamil had started to get a bad feeling.

"Jamil, right? What's that accent? You Australian?"

"No, my friend. I am not Australian, and you should know not to ask questions."

"Yeah, see, I got a problem, Jamil."

"Problems are not good. You do not want to have problems. You follow instructions and get paid, a lot of money. No problems."

"Sure, but here's the thing." They were driving down the I-20 frontage toward the intersection with the County Road 1130. "I done a few drug deals in my time, know what I'm saying? Since I was like fifteen. And I never done a deal like this. This is weird, and complicated, and I just keep asking myself, what the *hell* is going down here, dude? And I'm thinking, you know, this guy is called *Jamil? Seriously?* What is that, like some kind of Muslim name?"

Jamil had slowed at the intersection and turned west onto the County Road, thinking fast how he could defuse the situation. "Yes," he'd said, nodding, "it is a Muslim name. But this has nothing to do with Muslims or Christians or any of that. I might have been a Buddhist or a Jew. I am simply good at my job."

"So what's all this crap about 'pick up a suitcase in Los Angeles, get a Greyhound to Midland, someone will pick you up and take you to a hotel. You are already checked in.' What is this? Are we in some kind of James Bond movie?"

"What's the problem, Chet? You are not getting paid enough? Ten thousand dollars to take a suitcase from LA to Midland is a pretty sweet deal. You want more? That can be arranged."

At the next intersection he came off onto the highway that ran beside the railway tracks. Chet watched him in silence for a moment. "Yeah?" he said finally. "I dunno,

Jamil. You see one thing is sellin' dope. Somethin' different is betraying my country, see? I wanna know what's in that suitcase."

Jamil shrugged as he accelerated south toward the river. He smiled easily.

"I can tell you what is inside the suitcase. That is not a problem. Pure heroin, with a street value of many millions of dollars. Why do we have such an elaborate way of moving it? Because the DEA becomes more sophisticated every year, and the only way we can guarantee avoiding interception is by randomizing the process, so that it is impossible to know from one shipment to the next, who is going to deliver and where."

"Sorry, pal, I need to see with my own eyes that you have dope in that case and not some kind of bomb."

Jamil smiled and spread his hands. "That is not a problem either, my friend. In fact I admire your patriotism. But let me pay you first, and then we shall return to the hotel together and I will open the case for you. Will that satisfy you? And I will talk to my manager and see if we can increase your fee a bit. How is that?"

Chet nodded. "OK. I'm happy with that."

Jamil pulled over just past a track that led down to a farm and parked by the side of the road on a low bridge over a small river.

"It is here. I am afraid it is a little uncomfortable. We must go down beside the river."

"Are you kidding me? Why can't you just pay me here in the car?"

"Because I obey orders very strictly, Chet. It is attitudes such as yours that make operations fail. Please follow the instructions to the letter and all will go well." He got out of the car and went to the trunk. Chet did not get out. Jamil opened the trunk and withdrew a long dagger with a razor-sharp blade. He took that in his left hand and with his right he withdrew a Glock 17 from his waistband behind his back. Then he approached Chet's window.

"I am sorry, Chet. You are causing many problems by being obstructive. I do not want to shoot you. That is not the plan. But if you continue to be obstructive, in spite of my offers, you will leave me no option. Do you understand?"

Chet had raised his hands and had his eyes on the weapon.

"Take it easy there, Jamil." He tried a smile that didn't really work. "No need to get excited. We were just talking there. A loaded weapon is a dangerous thing."

"I am highly trained, Chet, in firearms and in knives. I strongly advise you to cease being obstructive and do as you are told. Now get out of the car and lead the way down beside the river along the right bank, among the cover of the trees. That is where I am instructed to pay you."

Chet climbed out and moved around the hood. He stepped over the low fence and backed up. Jamil followed after him, waving the gun and indicating for him to walk on beside the river.

They continued in this fashion for some two hundred yards, by which time they were surrounded by dense trees and the cold, clear water was spilling over rocks and making pools in the dappled shade. The right bank was encroaching now, but on the left bank there was a small, muddy clearing. Here Jamil said, "Cross to the far side."

Chet stepped shin-deep into the water, then paused.

"Where's my money, Jamil? I'm getting real nervous with all this bullshit."

"Your money is on the far side of the river, in that clearing. I put it there myself."

"So how come I don't believe you?"

"You are creating all of these problems yourself, Chet, by being uncooperative. Cross over and I will show you the money."

Chet turned and looked Jamil in the eye. Jamil hesitated, and maybe Chet saw something in his expression. Because he acted fast and explosively. He lunged forward, snatching at the barrel of the Glock with his left hand and smashing the blade of his right hand into Jamil's wrist. He wrenched the weapon from Jamil's fingers, but as he did so his feet slipped on the wet rocks and he fell backward into the water. He scrambled frantically. Water blinded him and covered his face so he could not breathe. Hard stones punched into his back as he thrashed and rolled over, struggling to get back to his feet. The gun fell from his wet hand. He erupted from the river, desperately wiping blinding water from his eyes, searching frantically for Jamil.

Jamil was no more than four feet from him, clutching at his broken wrist and his mangled fingers. He looked at Chet and there was insane rage in his eyes. He lunged forward, strangling a scream of fury in his throat, reaching with twisted, bleeding fingers for Chet's throat. But Chet was the product of the mean streets. He had been fighting since he could walk and he knew instinctively what to do when someone gets in your face. He acted without thinking. The heel of his right hand went to Jamil's jaw, forcing his head back. And his left fist drove hard and savage into Jamil's liver.

The pain was astonishing and Jamil gasped and doubled over. For a fraction of a second Chet thought about charging, seizing his advantage, beating the bastard down and drowning him. Maybe he should have done that. Maybe if he had done that things might have turned out different. But he didn't want a murder on his rap sheet, or on his conscience. So instead, seeing Jamil injured, unarmed, bent double and helpless, he turned and tried to run, wading knee-deep through the water.

It was a mistake. Jamil pulled the dagger from inside his jacket and, half-delirious in a world of pain and madness, he drove the long, slim blade through Chet's heart. Chet staggered two steps to the bank and collapsed facedown in the mud. Jamil had sufficient presence of mind to recover the blade and the Glock, and to take Chet's wallet as he had been instructed. Then he walked unsteadily upstream. He felt nauseous; the pain in his gut was crippling and reduced him to tears as he tried to walk. And his wrist, when he looked down at it, had swollen to twice its size, while blood oozed from his mangled fingers.

He cursed Chet for an awkward bastard. If he had just followed instructions. If he had just done as he was told.

He arrived at the car and half-fell behind the wheel. He slammed the door and weeping and sobbing, breathing with difficulty, he fired the engine and pulled away, not knowing where he was going or what he was going to do. He had just one thought in his mind. He needed to get somewhere where he could rest, tend to his wounds and recover from the blow he had received. He needed to get back to his hotel.

Chet's hotel. It was the only place.

He had booked two rooms, one for himself the day before, and the other for Chet today. It should not have mattered. When they found Chet he would be just another John Doe. There would be nothing to connect the body with Jamil. And by the time anyone noticed Chet had never returned to his room, it would be too late. It would all be over.

But it was like he had tried to explain to Chet. For that kind of plan to work you have to follow instructions precisely, or things start to go wrong. And his instructions had been to leave the hotel and not return; to eliminate Chet and drive immediately to Fort Bliss, stay in a motel and then make for San Diego. And that, he knew, was what he had to do. But he couldn't.

Not now.

He'd be lucky to make it to the Holiday Inn, which was just ten minutes away.

He did make it to the hotel parking lot and killed the engine. He pushed open the car door and as he climbed from the vehicle he vomited, and saw blood threaded in the bile. He wiped his mouth on his sleeve and walked unsteadily to the hotel.

He pushed through the door into reception and made it to the elevator without anybody noticing him. The elevator took an eternity to arrive, but when it did it was empty and he thanked Allah for that. Some instinct made him press Chet's floor. Let their attention focus on that room, not the room booked as Jamil. As he began to move up he felt faint. His head swam and he retched. But his stomach was empty and nothing came up except the taste of blood.

When he reached Chet's floor he practically fell out of the elevator, staggered down the hall, pulling the key from Chet's wallet, let himself into the room and fell on the bed groaning and clutching his belly. And ten seconds later he was up again, retching into the sink. This time there was more blood. He rinsed his mouth with water and pulled off his shirt. In the mirror he could see a bruise the size of a small melon. The blow had struck below the protection of the floating ribs and his fist had driven right into the liver and obviously ruptured it. Jamil knew that if he didn't see a doctor, he would die.

He went back to the bed and with trembling hands called the colonel. Her voice when she spoke was almost mechanical.

"Report."

"The room is booked, the case is in position and the target is eliminated."

"Good."

"But there is a problem."

"What problem?"

"I was injured."

"What injury? How did it happen?"

"He became suspicious of the arrangement. He did not want to go to the river. He did not believe we were trafficking narcotics. He thought because I was a Muslim it was terrorism."

"You are a Hindu!"

He suppressed a sigh of exasperation. "I am Indian, Colonel, but I am a Muslim."

"You should have told him you were Hindu. Nobody suspects Hindus of anything."

"Yes, Colonel. I offered him more money but he was still reluctant."

"So?"

"So in the end I was forced to pull a gun on him to force him to go down the river. But when I was going to eliminate him, he turned on me and attacked me. I killed him, but he delivered a blow to my liver and I think he has ruptured it. I am vomiting blood."

"Where are you?"

"In Chet's room."

"No! You can't stay there. You must leave. You must drive to Fort Bliss according to instructions."

"I can't. I can barely walk. If I try to drive that far I'll pass out on the highway. That will draw attention. I need a doctor. I think I am dying. He has ruptured my liver. I need help."

She was silent.

"All right. Stay where you are. I will get somebody to you who will take you to a doctor. Do not die in that room!"

She ended the call. He tried to lie down, but that made the pain and the nausea worse. So he remained perched on the edge of the bed. But even in that position the throbbing in his liver gradually became unendurable and he had to stand and walk about the room, which made him dizzy and nauseous. He had a panicky sense of spiraling down toward death. There was no position for him, no place, no angle at which he could place his body that did not result in steadily increasing pain and sickness. Twice he vomited and each time there was more blood. He was certain he was dying, and after half an hour he knew that he had no choice but to go to the ER. If he did the colonel would probably order him to be exterminated. But if he was going to die anyway, what advantage was there in staying put?

He was reaching for the phone to call 911 when there was a tap at the door. He stood with difficulty and made his way to open it. There was a man there with a leather jacket and very short hair. He was athletic and strong and Jamil knew with depressing certainty he was a hit man.

"Jamil?" Jamil nodded. The man looked him over. "You're in a bad way. We need to get you to a hospital. You left any blood anywhere?"

"No."

"Vomit? Any kind of DNA?"

"No."

"OK. Suitcase is in place?"

"Yes, everything is OK."

"All right, pal. I got the car downstairs. We'll get you a doctor and get you fixed up."

"But you are an exterminator."

The man put a smile on the side of his face. "And you're not? Come on, pal. I was in the area and this is an emergency, right? Just promise not to tell my union. Let's not waste any more time. Let's go."

He helped him to the elevator, down and across the lobby. Outside he had a Dodge Charger waiting and helped Jamil into the front passenger seat. He walked around the hood and got behind the wheel.

As they took off out of the parking lot Jamil asked him, "Are you going to kill me? I am dying anyway. Tell me so I can make peace with Allah."

"Relax, will you? You're a valued asset. The colonel told

me to get you to ER in Odessa. They have an asset there, OK?"

"OK," he said and let his head flop back against the headrest. "But if you decide to kill me. Please give me a moment to make my peace with God."

"OK, Jamil. I'll do that."

He pulled onto the I-20 and accelerated west, toward Odessa.

At exit 126 he took the exit, turned onto the overpass, then headed south, away from Odessa and into the country-side. And Jamil started to weep.

SIX

S OME HOURS BEFORE JAMIL HAD STARTED TO WEEP, and before I had settled to enjoy my second martini over Oklahoma, on my way back to DC, Maria and José had crossed from the small, Polish town of Terespol into the larger, Belarusian town of Brest, confirming thus that Europe does, in fact, have two Brests, but where one hangs free, the other is in the hands of the Russians. However, being Spanish, José was unable to appreciate this subtle fact.

Maria was asleep beside him as he handed over their passports. The guards, seeing they were European Union passports, waved them through. They crossed the Bug River and followed the road, which had an unpronounceable name four words long[1], as far as McDonalds, then turned left and crossed the River Mukhavets before turning right onto the Vulica Maskouskaja, a main artery which led them out to join the E30 which would, so José thought, lead them all the way to Minsk; and, he hoped, with as little delay as possible, all the way back to Malaga again. But, as they approached the intersection of the Vulica Maskouskaja, the E30 and the M1, Maria stirred, opened her eyes and pointed to the side of the road. "Pull over, would you?" she said, and smiled at him.

He checked his mirror. Saw the highway was pretty much empty and pulled into the side of the road.

"What's up? You OK?"

"Sure. I'd just like to drive for a while."

He spread his hands. "I've only been driving a couple of hours."

"Sure, I know." She opened the door and got out. "I just feel like driving. Come on, you can enjoy the scenery. It's beautiful here."

He sat a moment, staring at the wheel, not sure why he was unhappy. Finally he climbed out and stared at her. She avoided his eye and went to climb in.

"What's going on, Maria? Why are you behaving so weird? It's like I don't even know you. And all the while you're smiling, happy, no problem—but I can tell. You are shutting me out. What the hell is this about?"

"*Cari!* Ayyy!" She covered her face with her hands. "Nothing is wrong! What, I can't decide I want to drive the car suddenly?"

"Why are you so different?"

"I am *not* different! It's just the same old me! Now get in the car, will you?"

"No!"

"*What?*"

"I will not get in the car! I want to know what has happened to you! Why have you changed? This is not you! All of this!" He waved his upturned hands, trying to take in

Belarus, the car, his wife, their previous life and all the strangeness that had arrived to upset him. "*This! This!* Is not you! You have changed! It's like you've been abducted and replaced by an android!"

She took a deep breath and sighed.

"OK, José, I will tell you."

His face twisted with anxiety. "Is it another man? I hope you didn't bring me to Belarus to tell me you're in love with another man!"

She laughed. "No, silly! I am not in love with another man. It's nothing like that. Come and sit with me here."

She sat on the hood of the car and he came and sat next to her. The sun was declining in the west and the shadows of the woodlands beside the road were stretching long in the bronze light. A sudden breeze flapped her skirt and made him shudder. She slipped her arm through his.

"José, six months ago the doctors detected a tumor in my left breast."

"*What?*" He pulled away to stand in front of her. "Why didn't you tell me?"

"Because I didn't want to worry you."

He gripped her shoulders. "Maria, you have to share these things with me! How do you think that makes me feel? What happened?"

"They were able to destroy the tumor with ultrasound, but it took three months, and then we had to wait three months to see whether it came back or there was a metastasis. It didn't, and there wasn't. And, the very same week I got the news, I won the lottery." She giggled and shook her head. "It was like an affirmation of life. God was telling me to live! And so I thought, the thing I most wanted to do in the world was surprise you with this wonderful trip." She made a sad face. "But I see now I have been selfish and I have done it all wrong!"

Her face crumpled and she started to weep. He shook his head. "Nonono, *cariño!* No, you mustn't say that! It's just, you should have told me! Then I would have understood. That is what couples are for. We share and we support each other. I should have been there, helping you through the stress and the worry. Please, *please, cari,* tell me you will never do anything like that again."

"I promise, my love." She gave him a long kiss, then held his face and smiled into his eyes. "Now can we press on? I *really* want you to enjoy this trip."

"Of course," he said, "I promise."

They kissed again. Then, extricating herself from his embrace, she laughed and jumped behind the wheel. When he got in beside her she took off at speed down the road, heading east as though for Minsk, but after less than ten minutes she suddenly braked hard and, laughing out loud, she spun the wheel right onto a ramp, crossed over the highway and took off north along the P7 freeway.

He stared at her. "What are you doing?"

"I don't know!"

"*Cari,* where are you going? Minsk is east!"

"I know it is!" She laughed. "Let's live! We'll get lost! See what happens! It will be an adventure!"

"*Por dios, Maria!*"

She ignored him, accelerating fast through lush green countryside. They came to a town with a name in strange, Cyrillic writing. She barely slowed. She was like a crazy puppy that had been let off the leash. They thundered down Ulitsa

Kirova which ran in a virtually straight line for one and a half miles, bisecting the town, causing people to stop and stare as she hurtled past. They emerged at the far end of town into more lush, green fields and she began to accelerate again.

"The police, Maria," he said.

She smiled. She didn't even glance at the mirror. "Where?" she said.

"If they stop us. The police here are not like in Spain. Please slow down."

"You worry too much, José. Come on! This is a holiday. We are supposed to do crazy things."

"You said you want me to enjoy this trip, Maria. But I don't enjoy this crazy stuff!"

He could tell she was not listening to him. She did not even pretend to listen to him. Her eyes were on the road, scanning the verges, the scattered buildings and landmarks. Suddenly she began to slow. She muttered, "OK," and when he said, "Thank you," she glanced at him and grinned, as though enjoying some private joke: that he believed she had slowed for him instead of some other reason.

They had come to a small, un-signposted intersection. Here she turned right onto a narrow country road. They drove more slowly through fields for two or three minutes and came to a small village. She ignored the village and kept going. He was studying her face closely and said suddenly, "You know where you are going. How do you know where you are going?"

Her eyes were flicking left to right, taking in signs and features. She said absently, "I was here in a previous incarnation."

"Be serious!"

"I am."

They left the village behind them and she began to accelerate again, though not as recklessly as before. Tears started in his eyes and he half-shouted, "Maria! I want to know what is happening! If you continue like this I swear I will go to the nearest airport and get a flight back to Malaga! You are being *insupportable!*"

She slowed as the road curved sharply to the right. They passed a small village on the left and ahead of them was a huge forest, and a small, sprawling town with a sign that read, Orepichi.

She smiled at him and reached out for his hand. "*Cari*," she said, "I am not being nice, am I?"

"No! I am having a really bad time! I want to go home. I don't understand what has happened to you!"

They had come to the entrance to the village and she pulled over again into the long shade of three large trees. There she became serious, watching him as though she were examining his face.

"There are things about me I have never told you, *Cari*. You know nothing about my childhood or my teens, do you?"

Distress twisted his face. "Things? What kind of things? You never wanted to tell me. You said you didn't want to talk about it. Why are you doing this?"

"I am not Spanish, José. I have lived in Spain for many, many years. But I was not born in Spain."

"*Not Spanish?* What the—?" She didn't answer and incomprehension slid from his face, revealing astonishment.

His finger, as though of its own volition, rose and pointed out of the window. "You mean...?

She nodded. "I was born in Belarus. I have a flare for languages. I graduated from high school at fifteen and I went to Minsk to university where I got a degree in European languages. I am fluent in English and Spanish. At nineteen I moved to Malaga on a..." She hesitated a moment. "On a kind of scholarship from Moscow. I finished my studies, completely integrated into Spanish life, and stayed. A few years later I met you," her face contracted, "but I hated my past and I never wanted to talk about it."

He gripped her hand in both of his. "*Amor*, you said you would share..."

"And I am sharing, José, but you have to give me time and let me do it my own way. This is the town where I was born and I grew up."

He looked around, feeling strangely displaced, vulnerable, almost jealous of this small village that laid claim to so much of his wife that he had never seen or touched; that threatened him in a dark way he did not fully understand.

He looked at her suddenly. "You're not a *spy*, are you?"

She laughed that strange, new laugh of hers, leaned forward and kissed him. Then she fired up the car again.

"Are we going to meet your parents?"

"They are dead."

"Where are we going?"

"To see my uncle."

They moved steadily down the street, with the houses set well back among lawns and large front yards. It dawned on José that this was the only street, that beyond these houses there were just fields and forests. Finally, after maybe five or six hundred yards, they came to two identical houses, side by side on the right-hand side of the road. They were two-story houses, set fifty or sixty feet apart, painted pale blue with black, gabled roofs. They stopped outside the second house and she killed the engine. "This is it," she said, and after staring at it for a moment through the windshield, she opened the door and got out. He went to get out too but she said, "No, it's best that you stay here."

"Why?"

"These are very ignorant people. They don't understand."

"Understand what?"

"I will only be a few minutes. Please, just wait here."

She opened the gate to the front yard and walked quickly down the path, where she hammered on the dark blue door. It was opened almost immediately by a man in his forties. He was in shirtsleeves, smoking a cigarette. He let her in with no show of surprise, and closed the door behind her. José was aware that he felt sick. Anxiety was making knots in his stomach. He promised himself that as soon as she came out of the house they would find a hotel for the night and the very next day they would return to Spain.

And Maria would have to settle down. He circled around the thought a few times and concluded that he could not carry on with her if she continued with this new, bizarre behavior. He made it no more explicit than that.

Several hours seemed to pass, but when he looked at his watch he saw it was just five minutes. He told himself that if she was another five minutes he would damn well get out of the car and go and knock on the door. Or at the very least sit on the hood and smoke a cigarette. After the way she had treated him, lying to him and concealing the truth from him about so many things, and then ordering him to stay in the car, like he was some kind of second class-citizen who could not be seen in public. He checked his watch. Another five minutes had passed.

He thought about getting out and decided that ten minutes was not actually that long for a visit after all these years. He also decided he did not like the look of the man who had opened the door. He did not look like a peasant at all. And there was something else about him. He couldn't put his finger on it at first. He turned it over in his mind and realized it was the fact that the man had not looked surprised to see her. On the contrary. He had looked like he had been expecting her. And she had not seemed to explain anything to him. They had barely exchanged two words, she had stepped inside and he had closed the door.

He had been expecting her.

A strange sense of dread crept over him. For a moment he thought quite seriously about getting behind the wheel and driving straight back to Poland, leaving her here with her so-called family and her new, special friends. Then he realized she knew where he lived. She knew absolutely everything about him. And besides, he swore softly to himself and rubbed his face, she was his wife! He was getting infected by the craziness. The whole thing was getting to him.

He took a deep breath and told himself there had to be a perfectly simple explanation. She had probably phoned ahead and simply not told him about it. Nothing more to it than that. After all, she had told him practically nothing about the whole trip.

The door opened and she emerged carrying a suitcase.

She did not bid the man in the doorway farewell. He watched her struggle down the path and closed the door. She called to José, "Open the trunk!" He just stared at her. She repeated it, more emphatically, "Open the trunk! Help me, it's heavy!"

He picked up the key and pressed the button for the trunk. Then he got out and went to the rear of the car. She held the case out to him and he took it. It was heavy.

"What the hell is this, now, Maria?"

"Just put it in the trunk and I'll explain."

"More things you haven't told me?"

"Don't start."

"Don't *start?*" He put the case in and slammed the trunk closed. "Are you kidding me?"

"Just get in the car and don't make a scene."

Any answer was cut short because she climbed in behind the wheel and slammed the door. Anger flared up in his gut. He wrenched open the passenger door and got in beside her.

"Will you please tell me what that suitcase is?"

She turned the car around and headed back the way they had come. She didn't say anything. "I am telling you," he said, "that I have just about had enough! This is more than you can expect any man to put up with! You spring this nightmare trip on me out of the blue! You win sixty thousand euros—*Dios mio!* What we could have done with sixty thousand euros!—and instead of telling me, you buy this stupid car and arrange this nightmarish journey where all we do is drive and drive and drive! With you acting crazy all the time! Then you tell me this *insane* story about how you are not Spanish, and when we get to your 'uncles,'" he made the sign of inverted commas with his fingers, "house, a man is waiting for you there. He does not look surprised to see you, you barely exchange two words and then he gives you a damned *suitcase* to take away with you! Do you think I am *stupid?*"

She was driving at a steady, sedate pace. Dusk was falling and their headlamps came on. She glanced at him. "What is that supposed to mean?"

"Well what do *you* think it looks like? If I were doing this to you, what would *you* think? You are involved in smuggling for the Russian mafia! And you are going to get us both put in jail for the rest of our lives when we try to cross any one of the four or five borders we have to pass! That is, if you don't suddenly decide to go to China to visit your grandmother!"

"Have you finished?"

"No, not even close! But I will pause for now to listen to your fantastical explanation! As apparently now you are the sensible one and I am insane!"

"It is a tradition in Belarus..."

"*What?*" His voice became shrill. "It is a *tradition* in Belarus to give *half-ton suitcases to your cousins when they come to visit? You think I am an imbecile?*"

"It is a tradition in Belarus," she repeated quietly, "to give gifts of cheese and ham and other foods to family when they visit after a long time. My uncle is very old and a bit senile, that's why he didn't open the door, and he insisted on giving me..."

She trailed off, dispirited and aware he wasn't listening. Eventually José said:

"He was expecting you."

"I phoned to let them know I was coming."

"And you didn't tell me."

"I'm sorry."

"And all that theater on the road, 'be free,' 'explore,' 'get lost on an adventure...'"

"I said I am sorry."

"You have lied and lied and lied. I wonder if you have *ever* told me the truth about anything! How can I ever trust you again?"

He turned away, looking out at the evening landscape. She looked at him a moment, the back of his head, his neck and his shoulder that had become so familiar. She knew his smell, the touch, they were oddly reassuring. Then she looked back at the darkening road, but said nothing.

SEVEN

A BLACK LIMOUSINE HAD COLLECTED ME FROM THE airport and taken me through the first lights of the city at dusk, directly to the Pentagon. I had called Nero from the plane and told him I had a plan. I'd also told him it was the only plan that stood an ice cube's chance in a supernova, and he had arranged a meeting at the Pentagon with the director of the FBI, the director of the Secret Service and a senior presidential advisor on matters of defense.

I was led by a Pentagon official through rings E to B and finally came to the central plaza. From there we took an elevator to the seventh floor, where I was met by another official who led me to a large office with a view of the central plaza.

There was an oval table at the center of the room. There were three men sitting there, all of whom I recognized. One of them was the director of the Bureau, the second was the director of the Secret Service and the third was the president's advisor on national security. And then there was

Nero. He stood as I entered and said, "These gentlemen are not here, neither are we for that matter. Come in, sit down. The room is about as secure as any room could be and it has been swept for bugs and listening devices in the last fifteen minutes. These gentlemen who are not here and will not speak, can have no knowledge of your plan. Understood?"

I nodded and sat. "It's a good job they're not here then."

"Quite."

I didn't waste any time getting to the point. "Sir, the police chief of Midland, Texas said something to me which I have been turning over on the flight back, and which I would like to repeat to you."

"Very well."

"He said, 'Mr. Mason, seems to me you just don't know which way the blows are coming. There are three hundred and twenty-nine million people in this federation, and that many possible locations for your suitcase, *multiplied* by the number of places each of those people might have been in the last four or five days. I figure,' he said, 'that gives you roughly a billion places that suitcase might be. Hell!' he added, 'You got us lookin' in hotel rooms, but it might just as easily be buried in the roots of any of the trees where John Doe was found!'"

The three of them looked at each other and after a moment I said, "And of course he was right. Our response to this threat is totally ineffectual, and the odds of our finding and defusing the bomb before it blows are negligible. That means, realistically, the case will not be found and it will detonate, killing hundreds of thousands of people, possibly millions over time, and crippling the American economy beyond repair, allowing the Russians to move in and take over our economic and industrial infrastructure. This will happen in a matter of days and weeks."

The presidential advisor took a deep breath and looked at Nero. Nero shook his head and turned to me.

"I am assuming you did not ask me to arrange this meeting just so that you could depress us. You have a suggestion?"

I nodded for a bit. "Oh, yes, sir, I have. But I need to have you sufficiently terrified of the alternative before I present you with it."

"I think you may be sure we are sufficiently aware of the problem."

"Good, but just let me add that by the time the people in this room go on their summer vacations, American oil, all American banks, the railways and the Federal Reserve, to name but a few, will all belong to Russian oligarchs. In addition, at least one major city—probably DC, will have been razed from the map. That's like, the fifteenth of July, or the first of August. Six to twelve weeks."

"Your point has been made, Alex."

"Good, because the only way out of this situation—let me repeat that—the *only* way out of this situation, is to kidnap the senior military attaché at the Russian Embassy and make him talk."

"*Are you out of your mind?*" It was the presidential advisor, who wasn't there. For a man who wasn't supposed to be there he was on his feet and making a lot of noise, leaning across the table toward Nero and shouting. "This is what you brought me here for? To listen to this kind of stupidity? Have you any idea the kind of..."

He faltered because he saw too late where he was headed.

I wasn't feeling polite, so before Nero could lay into him with his own special brand of three-hundred-pound abuse, I said, gesturing at him, "This kind of what?" I turned to Nero. "This is the caliber of presidential advisors we get these days. No wonder we're getting shafted by a bear half our size!" I turned to the advisor. "Jerry, the outburst you had just now, that was stupid. There is no other word to describe it. Talking plainly, it was stupid. It was *stupid*," I said for the third time, enjoying the word, "and it was stupid because it was *unintelligent*. You can see with your own eyes that the United States is facing an *existential* threat. Do you know what existential means, Jerry? It means it is a threat to our very existence. It means we are looking at a situation where Washington DC, with you in it, will probably cease to exist *in a matter of days if not hours*. It means that in a few weeks we will probably have a puppet president installed who is controlled from Moscow. Are you assimilating these facts, Jerry? And your complaint to the director of intelligence networks is that my plan is a *risk!*"

I paused, laughed and shook my head. "Would you like to explain to me what *risk* could possibly be greater than the one I have just outlined? Would you please explain to me what *risk* is greater than an *existential* one?

"And if not, would you please explain to me a solution that takes into account both the nature of the threat—which is an atomic bomb—and the very limited timeframe within which we have to work? And if you can't do either of those two things, Jerry, would you please *sit down and shut up!*"

I turned to Nero and smiled, a thing he was fighting hard not to do.

"This," I said, "is why I wanted to terrify you, gentlemen. To avoid this kind of *unintelligent* reaction. We have a few hours, if we are lucky, in which to find a nuclear device which could be in a billion places. And that is only our first obstacle. Once found, any one of the six devices, real or dummy, could trigger the nuclear explosion. The task—and please try to assimilate this, gentlemen—the task is impossible. Which means it cannot be done." I paused to let it sink in. "So we have to go directly to the source of the information we need. The only way I know of doing that, short of invading the Kremlin, is to kidnap the chief military attaché at the embassy."

Jerry, who couldn't keep his mouth shut in a sandstorm, said, "Fine, do it, but there is no way the White House or the Pentagon can sanction it."

The other two just nodded their heads. Nero said, "Understood." To me he said, "Come," and we rose and left the room.

We followed the corridor to the elevators. Nero said over his shoulder, "Don't speak."

I was about to make a wiseass comment but he stopped me with his eyes. We went down to the parking garage and he led the way to a 1959 Rolls Royce Silver Cloud II. We climbed in the back and I saw that the driver's section was sealed off by a sheet of glass. Beyond the glass there was a driver who looked back at Nero. Nero waved his fingers in a "go, shoo" sort of gesture and the driver pulled away in total silence.

"Last decent car Rolls Royce ever made. Belongs to the Germans now of course—Rolls Royce, not this car—and they bring to it all the unimaginative, dull efficiency they bring to everything except beer."

"Can we speak freely here?"

"Of course."

"But not in the Pentagon?"

"Of course not."

"Right, foolish of me. So, we need to develop a plan to kidnap the Russian military attaché. And the first question that occurs to me is, will they have foreseen this move?"

"An excellent question, Alex, but I am certain that the answer is no. You saw how *Jerry...,* " he held the name up like a pair of soiled panties, "...reacted. That, I am afraid, is the standard mentality of the political administrator."

"OK, but this suitcase plot is pretty bold and subtle. There is at least one creative, imaginative thinker at work there."

"Oh, indeed, but I think we can be sure that whoever dreamed it up has been removed from the operation now and it is firmly in the hands of one of Putin's inner circle of maniacs. In any case, whether they have foreseen it or not, I agree with your exposition up there. I fear we have no choice but to do it. The answer is to do it in a non-telegraphic way."

We emerged from the parking garage into the Washington night and headed for the George Mason Memorial Bridge. Over the dark water he said to me, "We haven't the time to watch his movements and develop an elaborate plan. It must be simple, direct and unexpected."

"We can't jump him."

"No, certainly not. We have to lure him to some place and snatch him."

"I agree," I said, "but I've been turning that over in my head and the logistics and the mechanics of it become complicated to say the least. First of all, the only thing that is going to work at this short notice is something like an invitation to lunch or dinner from somebody so influential he won't suspect anything and he won't be able to say no, but anyone that influential is going to tell us to go to—"

"Me."

"What?"

"The influential person is me. If I ask the military attaché of any embassy to lunch with me or dine with me, they accept. At such short notice it will give an element of urgency to the matter which will make it that much more impossible to refuse. I will make it clear I want to discuss the REDS situation, and that I need assurances the Kremlin is not behind it. He will be instructed to attend and to give me those assurances. They know I have the president's ear, and they will want him to attend."

I thought about it a second and told him, "OK, that makes sense, but it takes us directly to the second problem."

"Which is?"

"You spending the next fifteen years in prison for conspiring to kidnap the Russian military attaché. The food in there is terrible. You'd never make it."

"But I am not going to kidnap him, you are. I will be clubbed senseless and you will make off with the attaché. You will take my car and I will not notice it stolen for hours."

"You want me to club you senseless?"

"Not especially, but it will make it more convincing if you do. As soon as I am *compos mentis* I will request the FBI and the metropolitan police to conduct a very thorough search for the Russian military attaché, naturally."

"Naturally. And where will he be?"

He looked down at his open palms, like he might be there. "I think, perhaps," he said, and then looked up at the passing city lights as we turned north toward New York Avenue, "I think you had better take this car. Nobody will dream of stopping it unless and until I report it stolen, and besides, it is on a special list which the authorities know to ignore. You will take it as far as North Bethesda, where you will abandon it in some parking lot and collect a car which will be waiting for you. It will be from the ODIN fleet, and after that..."

"But where will..."

"I am thinking, don't interrupt me."

We drove in silence up North Capitol Street and finally turned into Adams Street, where he dropped me at my door. I paused before climbing out of the car.

"Are you going to tell me?"

He eyed me a moment, then shook his head. "Be at the office tomorrow, nine o'clock sharp. Take the afternoon off, rest, have a good meal. The next couple of days are going to be very intense."

"Yes sir."

I climbed out and watched the magnificent old vehicle, armed with its V8 engine and two hundred horses, glide away under the trees toward 1st Street. I knew there was no point trying to second-guess him or predict what he was going to do. He was in a league of genius all of his own. The best thing I could do was take his advice and have a good meal and relax.

As I climbed the stairs and let myself into the house, my mind turned to a woman I had once had dinner with who was, probably, the most beautiful woman in the world. I had been about to invite her back to my place for a nightcap when Lovejoy had called and told me that Nero was on his way to collect me. That particular night had not ended well, but I wondered what she would say if I called her tonight. I told myself I would never know unless I called, found her number and dialed.

"Hey, stranger!"

I smiled. That was encouraging. "Hey yourself," I said, encouraging her back. "Have you forgiven me yet?"

"I could be mean and say, what for? But yes, it took a while, but it's nice to hear from you."

"I have been ordered by my boss—"

"The same boss?"

"The very same—to take the evening off and go out to dinner. He thinks I am overworked and overstressed. So I asked myself, who was the most beautiful woman I most wanted to go out to dinner with, and become unstressed with. Your name flashed instantly into my mind, as did your number."

"Your charm wouldn't work half so well if you weren't so damned good-looking, you know."

"Such hurtful words cut me to the quick. Shall I call for you in half an hour?"

"Bastard. Yes. But if you dump me again I swear I will never talk to you so long as I live."

"You have my word."

I hung up and the phone rang. It was Midland Texas PD.

"Chief Hanratty," I said, trying and failing to conceal the venom in my voice. "How can I help you?"

He answered with his slow, Texas drawl. "I hope I ain't catchin' you at a bad time."

"Not at all, just changing for dinner with probably the most beautiful woman in the world."

"I won't keep you, then. Just thought you'd like to know, we found another body."

I frowned. "A second body? Where?"

I climbed the stairs to my room and started pulling clothes out of my wardrobe while he took his time drawling.

"Down off the I-20, on the way to Odessa. The eleven seventy-eight that way takes you to the Midland Pines RV park. That's a popular spot for campers. But before you gets there, there's a big ol' pond. I mean it's more like a small lake, set back from the road a ways and concealed by trees. The body was found in there, by the water's edge."

I had managed an essential wash and to spray myself with deodorant while he took his sweet time with the buildup to Armageddon. Now I cut in and asked him:

"Any ID? Do you know who he was? I'm assuming it was a man."

"Oh, yeah, it was a man. Big guy, athletic build, short hair, military look about him. No ID. Nothin' on him at all. We took his prints and his DNA and we're runnin' them now. But I don't hold out much hope."

"What about the MO?"

"He was shot once in the belly and once right between the eyes with a 9mm pistol. We got the casings, so it was a semi-automatic. Totally different to the other one."

"Something went wrong."

"That's what I'm thinkin'. Damned if I know what, though."

"What about scene of crime officers? Footprints, tire tracks?"

"That place is full of tire tracks and footprints, but it looks like a medium-sized vehicle might have stopped there, and there were boot prints I think are a match for the ones at the river. Maybe they both do. We gotta look into it some more, but I thought you might want to know."

"I appreciate that. Chief. Any luck with the hotels?"

"You know how many people turn up in a town like Midland, book a hotel, go out to dinner and then stay over with friends? More'n you'd think."

I sighed. "Yeah, I guess."

"But we're on it. We'll find it. Y'all enjoy your night with your little lady."

I thanked him and hung up. While I pulled on clothes and splashed myself with aftershave, I visualized myself calling Nero and telling him about the unexpected developments in Texas. I heard his voice, sharp and peremptory. "I need you to go back and have a look. You can sleep on the plane. Observe and digest the scene. You can be back here for nine."

I examined myself in the mirror and applauded nature for making women like that kind of thing. And as I trotted down the stairs toward my car keys and my car, I reminded myself that Nero had stressed how important it was I have a good meal and a good rest. He had really underscored the importance of those two things.

So I stepped out into the night to do precisely as I was told.

EIGHT

In Moscow Colonel Alexandrina Vitsin sat motionless at her desk in her small office on Mokhovaya Street. The morning sun leaned through the east-facing window, laying patches of light on the floor, on the corner of her desk and on the east-facing side of her face.

Her black coffee grew cold on her desk.

Her hands rested, folded in front of her upon a manila file, the left hand on top of the right. Occasionally she swallowed, which gave her the appearance of a lizard. Repressed rage screamed behind her small eyes, battened down with steel control. Her black pupils contracted to pinpoints in her pale blue eyes, as though to hold the rage in.

There was a tap at the door. She said, "*Voyti!*" and the door opened.

Two men in suits came in. The older of the two, Zoltan Dulik, a man in his forties, had a broad Slavic face and powerful shoulders. The other, Captain Peter Belov, was a true Kievan Rus who had traced his ancestors all the way back to Sweden. He was six foot two with platinum hair, pale skin and dark blue eyes. And, thought the colonel as she watched him take his seat and cross one long leg over the other, he was full of that supreme arrogance of the true Rus. It was as though their languid eyes told you they carried their superiority in their Scandinavian blood.

Colonel Alexandrina Vitsin was not a Slav, and she was certainly not Kievan Rus. She was a mongrel. She had the look of a mongrel runt, with skinny arms and legs and a flat, bony chest, an unremarkable face and mouse-colored hair. She knew this, but she also knew she had the resilience of the mongrel, and the pitiless savagery needed to survive. She knew it, and the Kremlin knew it. Which was why this crazy plan had been placed in her hands. "If anyone can make it work," the president had joked, "Colonel Vitsin can!"

"How good is your English?" she asked the captain.

"Perfect," he answered quietly.

"How perfect?" she snapped.

He arched an eyebrow. "You cannot, by definition, qualify an absolute, Colonel. Perfect is perfect." He smiled, amused. "You cannot be almost perfect. But," he shrugged, "I was three years at Oxford and invariably scored As in my essays and dissertations. On one occasion I was forced to show my passport to a girl to prove I was not English. These are subjective judgments, Colonel, but we could score my English as convincing, if that helps."

Her hatred for the man moved in her veins like green poison.

"You will travel to Los Angeles." She tossed a large envelope across her desk to him. "Papers. You are Sebastian Fowls. Your backstory is there, memorize it. You are in California looking for property to buy. You have cards that give you access to two accounts in Panama. After the bomb detonates, you buy. Buy oil wells. You buy property in Texas in the Permian Basin, in the Western Gulf Basin and in Kentucky, West Virginia, Pennsylvania, New York, Maine, in the Appalachian Basin. You buy you buy you buy."

"I understand. What about the banks and financial institutions, and IT?"

"We will see. For now you focus on oil. You will report to Mr. Dulik."

Zoltan Dulik glanced at the younger man, who did not acknowledge him. "As you wish, Colonel."

"And you receive your instructions from him."

"Of course."

"There is another matter. The Pentagon has put what they are calling the Suitcase Affair in the hands of ODIN, the Five Eyes information network office. This is not what we anticipated."

Captain Belove spoke to the crease in his pants. "You believed they would put it in the hands of the CIA's Special Activities Center? But this is a hot potato that neither the FBI nor the CIA is equipped to deal with. The Pentagon will have chosen ODIN above the others, it is far better equipped and trained to deal with a problem this big."

Hot bile coiled in her stomach. "Thank you, Captain. It seems they have assigned Alex Mason to the task. He has issued a BOLO for unusual homicides, and has so far two police forces seeking the hotels where the homicide victims were residing."

Captain Belov nodded and gave a small shrug which

involved only his eyebrows. "That's good. It's what we wanted."

"Yes, but not so soon. It is going too fast. We do not want the cases found too soon. Also, Agent Alexandrovich has been killed."

The captain frowned. "By whom?"

"We presume by Jamil Abbad. He was assigned to eliminate Abbad. Now Abbad has gone missing."

"This requires an immediate result. I will have to delegate."

"Then delegate, but make it swift and make it convincing."

"Yes, Colonel."

She turned to Zoltan. "Equip the captain with everything he needs. Get him to Los Angeles. I want him on the ground as soon as it is humanly possible."

"Yes, Colonel. As you say."

"You may go."

He stood, clicked his heels and bowed. Captain Peter Belov smiled to himself: Zoltan Dulik, the civilian behaving like a loyal soldier. He stood, smiled at the colonel and gave a slight bow. "Colonel."

They left her as they had found her, with her hands placed neatly on the folder in front of her, immobile, staring with raging eyes at her own dark thoughts.

———

AGENT ALEXANDROVICH HAD FELT genuine pity for Jamil. They had sat there in the car a moment, with Jamil sobbing, his cheeks wet, rocking back and forth in what must have been excruciating pain.

"I am sorry," Alexandrovich had said. "The mission is too important, we can't have loose ends. You did a good job."

Jamil had not answered, he had simply curled in on himself and whimpered. Alexandrovich had climbed out of the car and walked around the hood. He had opened Jamil's door and taken hold of his arm.

"Come," he'd said. "Let's get it over with. At least it will stop the pain." As Jamil had climbed out, staggering slightly, Alexandrovich had smiled, not unkindly. "At least you have your faith, Jamil. You will go with Allah, as a brave warrior. I am an atheist. When my time comes I will go into the void and become nothing. But you, you have struck a decisive blow against the West. You will go to your seventy virgins in Heaven."

Jamil had looked weeping into his face. His voice was barely a whisper. "Please, take me to a hospital..."

"I am sorry. And I must use a blade. I cannot use a firearm." He shrugged. "We must be discrete. But I will make it fast and painless."

He paused and frowned. As so often happens with the brains of even the most highly trained special operatives, his was having problems processing what was happening, because it was unexpected and should not have been happening.

Jamil was swaying, as though he was about to fall to the mud. But he was holding a gun, a Glock 17 by the looks of it, and he should not have had a gun. And instead of reacting, Alexandrovich's brain was searching back for the moment when Jamil had acquired the gun. He never found it, because on the one hand he had not been there when Jamil had recovered it from the river, and in the second place because Jamil had shot him in the stomach with it.

He looked down to where the blood was oozing copiously from his belly. The pain was appalling. He became dizzy and the world seemed to lean away from him. The ground smacked him hard in the back and for a moment he was aware of the darkening sky above him. Then Jamil loomed over him and pointed the gun at his head. In a fraction of a second Alexandrovich wondered what he would find, if there was another world, how it worked and if his ancestors mattered at all. And did it matter that he was an atheist? At that instant something hard and violent crashed into his forehead, and Agent Alexandrovich ceased to exist.

Struggling to stay focused, Jamil wiped the Glock on his sleeve and his shirt, trying at least to smudge the prints, even if he did not wipe them off. Then he threw the weapon into the large pond. He turned and staggered back to the car and half fell behind the wheel, whimpering with the growing pain in his gut. It threatened to black him out, but he knew if he blacked out he would die. And one idea, one truth had become absolutely dominant in Jamil's mind. He did not want to die. They could give his seventy virgins to somebody else. He wanted to live. Even if he lived in prison, right now he didn't care. All he cared about was that he wanted to live.

He turned the car back toward Midland and drove recklessly fast back toward town. At the interchange he took the south loop going north, then took West Wall Street, honking the horn and accelerating to a hundred miles per hour, barely able to see what was on the road, as the piercing, stabbing pain glazed his eyes.

Finally, barely knowing what he was doing, he cut across the traffic on Garfield. He heard the screaming tires and the horns blaring but ignored them and followed the signs until he saw an ambulance staring at him and behind it a large door that said, "EMERGENCY."

The car collided gently with the front of the ambulance and stopped. For a moment Jamil sat outside the Midland Memorial Hospital in the dark, hemorrhaging internally and urgently in need of surgery. Semi-delirious, he wondered what to do. For some reason he was trying to remember how things had got so badly out of hand, as if that would help.

He opened the door and fell out of the car. He could hear shouts and running feet. People snapping questions and answers to each other. The clatter of small wheels. Then he was being lifted, legs and shoulders, and placed on a gurney. An angelic face looked down into his. She was concerned. She cared. She didn't know who he was or what he had done, but she cared.

"Can you hear me?" she was saying.

He frowned and nodded once. "It really hurts..."

"What's your name?"

Now they were moving, rattling toward bright lights. He said, "Jamil..."

"Can you tell me what happened, Jamil?"

He had a sense of racing, swooping. His eyes desperately wanted to close. His angel was saying, "Stay with me, honey. Jamil, you hang in there. We're going to fix you up. Can you tell me what happened?"

He found her with his eyes and she looked at him and

connected. He said, "My liver," then the words came as of their own volition. "I was mugged. They tried to mug me. Some guy hit me in the stomach. I've been vomiting, vomiting blood."

At that moment his eyes rolled and he became unconscious. The team immediately began to prep for emergency surgery for a ruptured liver, while the nurses began to strip off his clothes and a nursing assistant went through his pockets and his personal possessions, looking for identity documents and medical insurance.

His papers were delivered to the admin desk where he was admitted as Jamil Abbad, according to his British driver's license and AMEX card, and he was allocated a room. Then, according to procedure, the hospital telephoned the Midland Police Department and the switchboard forwarded the call to Detective Seth Macdonald because the fact that the victim had a British driver's license made it unusual. And unusual had become the buzzword.

"Where is he now?" he asked over the phone.

"He's in surgery. He says he was punched in the stomach, but the blow seems to have ruptured his liver."

"Is he booked into a hotel?"

"Yes, he's booked in at the Holiday Inn, on Crump Street." She gave him the number of the room. He grabbed his hat and his car keys, stepped out into the night and made the two-mile drive straight down South Big Spinning Street to the Holiday Inn in just under two minutes.

At the reception desk he found a very thin, pale young man with very large horn-rimmed glasses. He showed him his badge.

"How can I help you, Detective?"

"Jamil Abbad booked a room here."

The receptionist rattled at his keyboard and after a moment nodded. "Yes, Detective, that is correct."

"Has he slept here?"

The receptionist frowned at him like he thought he'd seen a glitch in the matrix. "Well, he booked the room yesterday and I'm pretty sure he slept here last night. Then he came in a little earlier, looking *very* drunk, and went up to his room. Then a while later a man came, and they left together. Mr. Abbad still looked very drunk. And I haven't seen them since."

"What was this other guy like?"

"Big, tall, leather jacket, very short hair."

"I'm going to need a key to his room."

"Yes, Detective." He reached for a card and slipped it into a programmer, talking all the while. "But the odd thing is, you see, he booked two rooms. I'm mentioning this because of what you asked me, had he slept here. Because, you see, he booked the other room, his friend showed up to check in late this morning, took his luggage up, went out and hasn't shown up since. It was booked *by* Mr. Abbad, *for* a Mr. Chet Baker."

"Get me keys for both rooms." He pulled his phone from his pocket and dialed a number. "Chief. I think we have the room. I am going in now on probable cause, but let's get a damned warrant anyway just to cover our asses. We have a British guy in surgery now with a ruptured liver, and we have him leaving his room at the hotel with a man matching the description of the second body. We also have a second room booked at the hotel by this Brit in the name of Chet Baker. Only Chet Baker never showed. Most probably because he was lying facedown in the mud by the river." He paused for a moment, listening. Then said, "Yes sir, and we'd best get the crime scene boys here to go over the rooms, and maybe you'd best notify Mason in DC."

He hung up and eyed the receptionist. "Show me Abbad's room first, then Chet Baker's."

He found Jamil's room as Jamil had left it, untouched since the cleaners had been in. He snooped around for two minutes and, satisfied there was nothing there of interest he said, "OK, show me Baker's room."

Chet Baker's room was a different story. The first thing he found was the blood in the sink and in the toilet. Then he found the long-bladed dagger on the floor. By that time he was hearing the sirens arriving outside. He waited for the uniforms and the crime scene officers to disgorge from the elevator and collared a sergeant, pointing at the ceiling and then at Chet's door.

"You got a room upstairs. This is the key. Seal it till the crime scene boys are through with it. This room here, you seal that too and don't let nobody in there neither till crime scene boys have been over it with a fine-toothed comb. Joe!" He pushed past the sergeant and collared a man in a white plastic hazard suit. "You got vomit and blood in the sink and in the can. The guy is traveling on a British passport. I wanna know who he is. Obviously check CODIS and AFIS, but get the Brits to check their databases too."

"You got it, Detective."

"Now everybody just wait out here while I go and check somethin'."

He reached in his pocket, pulled out some latex gloves and snapped them on. He went back into the bedroom. He glanced briefly at the bathroom again and noted the blood and bile. In the bedroom he saw the bed was made but rumpled, where someone had lain on top. He went to the wardrobe, and with a cold prickling on the back of his neck he opened the doors. The cold prickling crawled all over his skin and his heart pounded once, hard, high in his chest. There was a bar with hangers, and below it a low set of built-in drawers. Placed on top of these drawers were two red Samsonite suitcases.

NINE

NERO LIVED ON 35TH STREET NW, IN A LARGE, Victorian brownstone that would have looked at home in Manhattan. It was on three floors and had a large basement. It had a tower with a conical, black slate roof, a balustraded balcony and beneath that a large porch with Greco-Roman columns. In designing the small front yard, which was really a small garden, the architect had suddenly departed from sixteenth-century fairyland and wound up in the early Middle Ages, so that everything was made to look like rough-hewn stone. Some would call it eclectic, others simple bad taste. Give it another hundred years and they would call it something like late 19th-century American neo-Gothic and raise the price three hundred percent.

He had brought me here from the office, and as we climbed down from his Rolls he stood staring at the building for a moment. "It is grotesque," he said, "but it has character and charm." Then he turned and scowled at me.

"You may feel privileged. Nobody has ever been here before."

I gazed at the pile, and then at Nero, who was still scowling at me.

"Thank you, sir. I will try to remember it was not my charm, but the threat of nuclear annihilation that made you invite me."

"You are trying to be witty," he said and climbed the stairs. The door seemed to open of its own volition and I followed him into a cool, shaded hall that was the size of some people's houses. The floor was a mosaic of brown and amber marble, and a mahogany staircase that was a work of art in its own right ascended on the right in a broad curve. At the foot a huge, arched oak door stood open onto a large drawing room.

Lucas, Nero's manservant, was holding the door and muttered, "Good morning, sir. Should I prepare a third setting for luncheon?"

"No, Mr. Mason will not be lunching with us. Coffee in the drawing room, Lucas."

Lucas closed the door, took our coats and we disappeared toward the kitchen. We moved into the drawing room. It was a man's drawing room. You can get sent for rehabilitation in Alaska for saying things like that these days, but it was a man's drawing room. It was all mahogany, oak and dark leather, and smelt richly of furniture wax and pipe tobacco. Sure, a woman can have a drawing room like that, but then she's just a woman with a man's drawing room.

He gestured me to a chesterfield that was set by the fireplace and moved toward what looked to me like a Jacobean credenza.

"A shot with the coffee. Will you have Cognac, Armagnac or whisky?"

"Whisky, thank you sir."

"The military attaché, who is called General Nikolay Sidorov, with the accent on the 'I,' will arrive at twelve noon, ostensibly for drinks and a chat before luncheon at one. I have insisted that we must be completely alone, and I have agreed to let his men scan the ground floor to ensure that there are no listening devices. That should take no more than ten or fifteen minutes."

He placed a cut crystal shot glass of whisky on an occasional table beside me. Then he sat in the chesterfield opposite as the door opened and Lucas entered bearing a silver tray of coffee. When he had poured, distributed and left, closing the door behind him, Nero continued.

"We shall then sit and I shall approach him on the subject of the suitcase and the spurious Russian Executive for the Dissemination of Sovietism. He will assure me that they are as much an enemy of Russia as they are an enemy of the West. We will wrangle and I shall try first to make him see sense, and then I shall try to bribe him. By this time, say thirty minutes after his men have left, and at fifteen minutes before one, you will come in, in a balaclava, brandishing a gun."

"Where have I been till then?"

"In the cellar. We will have a look now, in a while. I will make a show of defying you and you will knock me out. Make it convincing. I used to box and wrestle in my youth. I have a strong chin."

"I'll do my best. He may have an electronic alarm to call his men."

"I have thought of that. We will be jamming any incoming or outgoing messages for the duration of the visit. You will then sedate him and take him down to the basement. I have a special, concealed room down there that is controlled from the fuse box. You lock him in and you leave by the garage at the back. You take the Rolls Royce and you drive it, as we have said, to North Bethesda."

"I don't take the general with me?"

"No, you leave him downstairs, locked in the room. You deposit the Rolls at the Montrose Crossing parking lot on Nebel Street. There, outside the A.C. Moore arts and crafts store, you will find a silver Toyota station wagon with this license plate." He handed me a slip of paper. "Nobody will be looking for it and nobody will associate it with you or with me. You will return here, park the station wagon on Volta Place, and leave the keys in the glove compartment. You will then walk here without hurrying, and you will enter via the alley on Dent Place, and the gate to my backyard."

"Does Lucas know about this?"

"You and I know about this. Nobody else."

"What if he—"

"He has instructions to set out a buffet luncheon in the dining room and leave no later than twelve thirty, via the kitchen. He will see nothing and he will hear nothing."

"It's tight."

"It has to be tight and it has to be clockwork. Now, by the time you return I will have come to and telephoned the police. Clearly if you arrive and the place is crawling with policemen, you simply play along. I have called you and this is a matter in which we and the Metropolitan Police Department will cooperate. Once they are gone you go down to the basement and interrogate the general. He must at no time identify you or the place where he is being held. He can suspect all he pleases, but he must have no proof."

"We'll have to make him talk very quickly. This could trigger an attack."

"I know. That's a risk we have to take." He looked at his watch. "Time to act. Take your glass and your cup to the kitchen. Lucas will show you the cellar."

The cellar, or basement, was on two levels. The first level was the kitchen and pantries, which took up the whole of the floor area of the house and included a small dining room, a sitting room and a bedroom and bathroom. I gathered this was where Lucas lived. He thanked me for the glass and cup without enthusiasm and unlocked a door in the kitchen wall for me.

I went down alone. There was a flight of stone steps forming a dogleg into a kind of catacomb of arches and domes. Several of the walls were taken up with racks of bottles. I inspected a few and was not surprised to find mainly claret, followed by Burgundy, Ribera del Duero and Rioja. There were also racks of port, cognac, champagne and whisky, Scotch and Irish.

Opposite the wines there was a bare brick wall. Standing at a skewed angle to it was a long, refectory table which I gathered would normally be pushed up against the wall. By the color of the wood and the workmanship, I figured it must have been three hundred years old if it was a day. It held cases of glasses, a couple of corkscrews, thermometers and various other utensils someone like Nero would use while choosing a wine.

The table had obviously been shifted. You could tell that

not only from the dust marks on the floor, but from the fact that the wall stood open a few inches. There was a door cunningly concealed in the brickwork that, when closed, would be completely invisible to the eye, because the shape of the door itself followed the pattern of the bricks. Beside this door, bold as brass, was the fuse box. And in the fuse box were two switches, one that opened and closed the door, the other which supplied or denied power to the cell beyond the door.

I approached it and looked in. There was a bed which looked reasonably comfortable, a table and two chairs. In a small annex there was a bathroom.

There was also, standing in the middle of the floor, a motorized hydraulic gurney, and lying on it were a dart gun with six tranquilizer darts, a pair of latex gloves and a balaclava.

As always with Nero, everything had been foreseen.

Or so I thought.

I prepared everything I was going to need and put it where I was going to need it, then went up to the kitchen to wait while Lucas carefully ignored me. At noon sharp there was a ring at the doorbell and Lucas went to open the door. There was a murmuring of voices, low rumbles redolent of icy steppes, vodka and howling lone wolves.

For ten minutes after that I heard the tramping of feet back and forth, and eventually the filing of men out the door. The door closed. It was twelve fifteen and Lucas came back to the kitchen and started transporting plates of cold ham, roast beef, chutneys and cheese to the dining room, along with hot rolls, butter and a bucket of cold beer. My stomach told me it was a shame it wasn't going to get eaten (and drunk). I told my stomach not to jump to hasty conclusions.

At twelve thirty Lucas left via the kitchen door. I pulled on the balaclava and the gloves, armed myself with the tranquilizer gun and stormed into the drawing room. Both the general, a portly man with long gray hair and a well-cut suit, and Nero stared up at me in astonishment. For no particular reason I snarled in a Russian accent.

"No move!"

The general struggled to his feet, bellowing, "*Kak ty smeyesh?*"

I had no answer for him but fortunately Nero was on his feet with surprising speed and took a vicious swipe at me with a huge hand propelled by three hundred pounds and five hundred horsepower. I leaned out of the way, stepped in and smacked him hard in the mouth, busting his lip and bruising his jaw so it would look good. He fell with a phenomenal crash onto a Queen Anne occasional table and turned it into three-hundred-year-old matchwood.

I didn't pause in my atrocities. I turned and shot the general in the chest. He stared down at the dart and, perhaps through the power of suggestion, he too keeled over backward, though fortunately he did not destroy any priceless antiques on the way down.

I checked his heart to make sure he wasn't dead, then sprinted back down to the basement. I grabbed the gurney and wheeled it at speed to the drawing room, where I collapsed the legs and laid it next to the general. I rolled him onto it with difficulty and raised it up. Then I ran him back to the basement and wheeled him with even more difficulty down the steps and across to his cell. Once there I dumped him on his bed, stepped out of the cell and locked him in.

So far, so good. I checked my watch. I had exactly five minutes in which to make myself a hot crusty roll with ham, cheese and chutney, and down a cold beer. I did it in four and sprinted out, belching softly, to get the Roller.

Before the Woke Revolution decided to make fun illegal in case it offended some miserable bastard, a famous brand of vermouth ran a series of advertisements based on the idea that only beautiful people were allowed to drink that particular brand of vermouth. The 1959 Rolls Royce Silver Cloud II is the motorized version of that vermouth. And, not coincidentally, you will find that particular brand of vermouth in the onboard bar in most Silver Clouds, right next to the Dom Perignon. It is silent, smooth, elegant and, with a two hundred and thirty horsepower V8 engine, it was pretty powerful too.

I drove sedately, though I knew that the license plate was on a list that, if ever it was radioed in, it would raise a flag to let it pass and not interfere. Even so I preferred not to tempt the gods and kept within the speed limit.

It was a ten-mile drive and it took me fifteen minutes to get there and park outside the Giant supermarket. I left the car there and had a stroll across the lot trying to be gray and unnoticeable. After a couple of minutes I found the silver Toyota station wagon. I checked the license plate, confirmed it was the right car and climbed in. Then, feeling far less exquisite, I retraced my steps back to DC.

The drive was uneventful and at a little after two thirty I pulled into Volta Place and parked the car by the steps. I popped the key in the glove compartment, climbed out and strolled through the leafy, suburban streets up toward Dent Place. That was when my telephone rang. It was Nero.

"Sir."

"Alex, there has been an incident."

"What kind of incident?"

"I want you to stop what you are doing immediately." I stopped walking, found a London plane tree and leaned against it, facing the terrace of houses that lined the road. "I'm afraid I have had a home invasion. The brute knocked me unconscious and kidnapped my guest. The police are here, the commissionaire is on his way and so is the director of the FBI. Lucas had left and the animal who attacked me must have known I was alone. Fortunately Lucas returned because he had forgotten to chill a particularly good Chablis I intend to have tonight with grilled salmon and fennel root."

"Son of a gun, what a thing to forget."

"Quite. In any case, there is nothing for you to do until I have finished speaking with the commissionaire and the director. I'll call you."

"So this guy who laid you out, sir. He must have been a pretty tough, athletic guy, you having such a strong jaw an' all."

"You are trying to be witty again, Alex. In fact he was a puny, scrawny fellow, but he caught me off guard."

"Right. OK, well, you call me if you need anything."

"Rest assured I will."

So I changed direction and took a walk west, to Wisconsin Avenue. There I wandered uphill till I came to a small coffee shop. They had a couple of chairs and tables outside, but I didn't feel like being visible, so I sat inside and had a coffee and a cheese and ham sandwich wile I watched the news on the television on the wall. They were discussing the suitcase bombs. It seemed to be about the only subject you could find on the TV or the radio these days.

A well-known anchor was sitting at a round table with an expert on the stock exchange and my friend Jerry, the presidential adviser on defense, and he was asking the questions, "Does this constitute a real threat, and how is it impacting Wall Street?"

"Mike, the short answer to your question is yes. That is exactly what it is, a threat. But it is an uncorroborated threat which so far has proved to have absolutely zero evidence to back it. Let's face it, until now, nobody had ever heard of the Russian Executive for the Dissemination of Sovietism, but now these unknown terrorists have access to nuclear devices?" He shrugged. "Is it a threat? Yeah, if a guy comes up to you in the street with a gun and says, give me your watch or I'll shoot you, that's a threat. But if a guy who is falling over drunk comes up to you and tells you he's got a gun in his car and he's going to shoot you if you don't buy him another drink, that is also a threat. How credible is it? That is another question."

The interviewer turned to the other guest. "Bob, when this story first erupted in social media, the fear was that Wall Street would implode because of fears that the American economy itself was going to implode—or explode, as the case may be. Yet that doesn't seem to have happened."

"No Mike, it hasn't, and few people on the inside believed it would. I think the perception within the financial community is that this has been, as Jerry implied, at best a hoax, at worst an attempt to destabilize the economy and create financial opportunities for sharks. But again, as Jerry pointed out, there has been absolutely no material evidence to show that there is anything behind this other than very irresponsible scaremongering. And patently REDS does not exist as a terrorist organization. Nobody has ever heard of them."

Mike turned back to Jerry. "So, I mean, how worried should we be? Are you telling us that the security services are simply shrugging their shoulders and ignoring this threat of a nuclear device? Surely 9/11 taught us we should not be complacent about our national security."

"No, not at all, not at all. The FBI and other security agencies, along with the state police departments, are *very* actively investigating this threat. But as I say, to date, we have no indication that this is anything other than a hoax."

I glanced at my phone, wondering how long Nero was going to be. In the background I could hear Mike the anchor saying, "Oh, hold on, we are getting this in from Midland, Texas. We are going live right now to Marisa, our correspondent on the ground..."

I looked up to see an apocalyptic image of the city of Midland dwarfed by a massive column of black smoke and fire. Marisa's voice was raised over the sound of people shouting and screaming in the background.

"Mike, there is nothing but confusion here, but what I am being told is that a suitcase *was* found at the Holiday Inn. I repeat, a suitcase *was found* at the Holiday Inn, and that a member of the Midland Police Department opened it. We do not know, I repeat, we *do not know* if the explosion was as a consequence of that, and most worryingly, Mike, we do not know if the explosion was nuclear..."

TEN

I called Nero.

"Are you watching the news?"

"We have just heard."

"Get them out of there."

"I am in the process. I'll call you."

I paid at the counter and started making my way along Dent Place. Halfway there he called.

"I told them to stop wasting my time. The explosion in Texas leant weight to my argument. Come through the alley to the parking lot in back. You'll find a gate to my backyard."

I hung up, followed his instructions and five minutes later I was descending the mossy limestone steps to his kitchen. Lucas let me in with his usual face which said he could not really see me, and gestured toward the passage that led to the hall and the drawing room. I ignored him as courteously as he ignored me and made my way quickly to where Nero was standing in front of the cold grate going up and down on his toes and twitching his nose.

"This is not an atom bomb," he said as I walked through the door.

"How do you know?"

"If it had been they would have ensured the damage was far greater. No, this was a thermobaric charge strategically placed near or upon a gas tower or a pipeline. This was a message."

"If you look for the bomb you will trigger more explosions, and the next one could be nuclear."

"Precisely."

"I have to talk to Sidorov."

"Be my guest. I shall not accompany you. I do not even know you are here. I just ask that you spare a thought for the forensics."

"I am only going to talk to him—for now."

I retraced my steps to the kitchen, carefully ignored Lucas and trotted down the stairs to the basement. There I pulled on the balaclava and the latex gloves, fished a pencil flashlight from my pocket and killed all the lights. Then I opened the door to the cell and shone in the flashlight.

For a moment I was struck by how pathetic a figure he cut. He was suddenly an old man, cowering on a bed and shielding his eyes. He should have been sitting in front of an open fire with grandkids on his lap and asking to be read stories. Instead he was locked in a cell, about to be threatened with the most gruesome torture imaginable.

I pulled up a chair and sat, keeping the light focused on his eyes.

"The bomb exploded in Texas." He blinked a few times but said nothing. "So the message is, if we search we detonate bombs. One of those might be nuclear. We don't know how many megatons, but with modern technology we know it could be massive."

I paused. He still didn't say anything, but shielded his eyes from the light.

"We are perhaps minutes, perhaps seconds, from a nuclear blast that will kill hundreds of thousands of my people, perhaps millions, and at the very least will cripple the Western economy and make the USA a puppet state of the Kremlin." A short pause and I went on. "Now, I want you to consider this question, how far do you think I will go to stop that from happening?"

Now he looked over at me. He tried to hide it but he looked scared.

"I am not going to waterboard you, General. I am going to vivisect you, and post photographs of you all over social media, so your family will see them. I am a sadist, General. I enjoy seeing people suffer. I have been selected for this job. And let me assure you that, under the circumstances, Amnesty International is not going to come rushing to save you, or interrupt our conversation. This is really not worth your while."

I switched the flashlight off. In the silence I could hear his breath trembling. I gave it a count of five and switched it back on again.

"I am going to go and get my tools now, General. I'll be back in about fifteen minutes. Then I am going to remove your right foot without anesthetic. Don't worry, we have the best medical facilities to ensure you don't die...," I paused, "and if you pass out we can revive you almost immediately.

We will then proceed to your knee." I stood. "Believe me, General, no human could endure it. Your wise choice is to start cooperating before you suffer any unnecessary losses."

I closed the door and flipped on the lights, but left him in the dark. Then I trotted up the stairs to where Nero was staring out the window looking vaguely sick.

"What did you do? Don't tell me. Did he talk? What did he say?"

"I told him I was going to vivisect him and I told him he had fifteen minutes to think it over while I went to get my tools." I took a deep breath. "I'm hoping he'll break before it becomes necessary to prove I am serious. But if he's a real tough nut it may become necessary to convince him we mean business. Do we have anyone who will do that?"

"I'm afraid so." He sighed. "I'll have a word with the brigadier at COBRA. They are discreet, and ruthless."

I frowned. "COBRA?"

"Never mind."

"Well, you'd better give them a call. We need somebody talking to him and wielding a pair of pliers. I am not the best man for the job, plus I need to get back to Texas and find out exactly what happened there. Whatever it was, we don't want it happening again."

He nodded. "Agreed. From what I am hearing, there has been no radiation detected so far. Take the jet. I'll have Lovelock call and ensure it is ready for you."

I got a cab to the airport and called Chief Hanratty on the way.

"Yeah, what?"

"It's Mason."

"I know who y'are. What do you want?"

"Is Macdonald alive?"

"Why the hell shouldn't he be?"

"I'm on my way from DC now. They tell me it's a three-hour flight. I'm going to try and make it in two. And I am going to want two things when I get there, Chief. First I want a full and detailed report on exactly what the hell happened. And second I want somebody to explain to me exactly what part of 'don't touch it' the Midland Police Department had a problem with."

He was very quiet, then said, "OK, I'll have Macdonald collect you at the airport."

"Do that."

At the airport I showed the pilot my Office of the Director of Intelligence Networks card which said I was attached to the Pentagon and told him, "I need you to do everything in your power to get me to Midland, Texas in two hours. I know this bird will give you seven fifty. Just try not to blow up on the way. We've had enough explosions for one day."

He smiled. "We'll make it, sir."

On the plane I watched the news. The New York, London and Tokyo stock markets were in free fall. The Federal Reserve had as yet not made a statement, but that didn't surprise me as there was sweet Fanny Adams they could say. But everything the Federal Reserve wasn't saying the Pentagon and the White House were saying. There was no evidence that the explosion was related to what they were now openly calling the Suitcase Hoax. The explosion had been a freak accident and was not a nuclear detonation.

Japan and London both weighed in assuring investors there was nothing to worry about, though Brussels was more muted and merely called for caution. I smiled without much humor. Germany and France, the true powers behind the EU, both knew that if the USA fell, they were the heirs apparent to the status of Western superpower.

Heaven knew the Pentagon and the White House was no White Council of enlightened saints, but I wondered if a Free World led by the European Union would not be just a little bit darker and more dystopian. Who knew?

The pilot was as good as his word and two hours after takeoff we were circling above Midland, where a column of black smoke half a mile wide and several miles long was trailing east across Greenwood toward Forsan, Elbow and Big Spring. Ten minutes later we touched down. When the stairs were lowered I thanked the captain and told him, "Hang around. I don't know how any of this is going to play out. But I'll be needing you sooner rather than later."

As I trotted down the steps I saw Macdonald driving across the tarmac to meet me in a dark green convertible Mustang from the time when flares and sideburns seemed like a good idea. He pulled up in front of me. I climbed in and told him, "I am as mad as hell."

"I know y'are, and so am I. Life sucks. Now why don't you keep quiet a while and let me tell you what happened?"

We pulled out of the airfield and headed south on A Street. Most of the southern and eastern sky was a black sheet of oily smoke belching from the processing plant outside town, by the Sibley Nature Center.

Macdonald spoke slowly, thumping out the syllables with his palm on the steering wheel. "*There-ain't-no-radiation-detected!* I do not know what this is. We need to get teams in there to investigate exactly what caused this, but that ain't going to be possible for days, maybe weeks. That was one *hell* of an almighty explosion! That was six miles from the department and it rattled all the goddamned windows. We have critical victims in hospital who were three miles from the blast. And thank the good lord the wind is blowin' away from town. Otherwise I don't know what we'd a' done. Right now—" He pointed east and south through the windshield. "Right now they're evacuatin' Greenwood and Stanton, and Foresan is on standby.

"Now, I don't know how they done this, Mr. Mason. And we won't know until we can get personnel in there to analyze the damage. But what I *can* tell you is, it ain't nuclear."

"You don't know how they did it? I'll give you a thumbnail sketch. You can be pretty sure they placed one or more thermobaric charges on a number of the gas towers and turned the whole damned processing plant into one big bomb. And *that* was somehow detonated by the suitcase."

He pointed at me, eyebrows high. His voice was tight.

"I do not know that! Nobody has proved that! You just hold your horses till I tell you what happened."

We were downtown, moving among massive office blocks and towers of steel and glass. There were no people on the streets. It was like the apocalypse, and ahead, between the huge buildings, all you could see was the black sky.

"'Course, you don't know about any of this," he said, and stared at me frowning.

"Know what?"

"Jesus! OK, from the top: we get a call from the Midland Memorial. Some British guy has admitted himself to hospital because he has a ruptured liver. He says he's been mugged and the mugger has busted his liver. So the hospital calls us and we go down and, long story short, turns out this guy, Jamil Abbad, has booked two rooms at the Holiday Inn."

"Who was the other room for?"

"Chet Baker."

We turned onto Big Spring and hurtled down for a mile before making the tires complain turning into the Holiday Inn parking lot. We stopped outside the entrance and the tires complained about that too. As we climbed out and pushed our way into the hotel he continued talking.

"So we go to his room and there's nothin'. It's pristine. We go to Chet's room and there's blood in the sink and in the toilet. There is also, and get this, a long-bladed dagger on the floor. So I figure this is the guy who killed the beach boy, right? Only maybe the beach boy had something to say about it and busted his liver first. Forensics will confirm it, but that's how I figure it. So far we have compared the prints in the room with the deceased's prints and it's pretty certain our John Doe is Chet Baker."

"That's good."

"Right."

We climbed into the elevator and rode it to the second floor. There we got out and he led me to Chet Baker's room. It was sealed with yellow tape but the door was open. We ducked under and went in.

"Anyhow, I have 'em seal both rooms, but before I let the crime scene boys go to work, me and a sergeant go into Chet Baker's room, and I tell her to be real careful and touch nothing. Just like you said. Just put up the tape and seal the room, right? So she's doin' that and I open the wardrobe."

As he said it he did it and gestured with both hands. I looked and saw two red Samsonite suitcases.

"Did I touch 'em? Yeah. When you said 'Don't touch 'em' I thought you meant don't open them. That was my mistake and believe me, I feel bad. What did I do? I picked up the top one to look at the catches and see if there was any prints on 'em. Then the whole goddamn town shook."

"You picked up the case and you peered at the latches..."

"Like this." He made like he was picking up the case in two hands, raised his arms and bent forward. "And *bam!* I'm tellin' you boy, the glass in the window rattled. And this is triple glazing."

"Do it again. Don't pick up the case but repeat the action."

He did it again and I timed him on my stopwatch. "Three seconds. More than enough time for a motion sensor to trigger a cell phone message to a detonator. That really screws things up. Have you called the Feds?"

"They have a team on their way from the Austin field office. Should be arriving about now."

"We don't know how many detonators are active in that case. Triggering one could activate another. So you move the case a second time and it detonates a second bomb." I ran my fingers through my hair and for a moment had the feeling I was losing my grip on the situation. Then I reminded myself I'd never had a grip on the situation in the first place and felt better. "What about this British guy, Jamil Abbad?"

"Last I heard he was in surgery."

"I want him guarded at every instant. I want two cops sitting on him when he's in the can. I want him controlled at every moment, and as soon as he can speak, I want to talk to him. Have you sent his prints to Scotland Yard?"

"Yes. So far they have no hits."

I Called Nero.

"Report!"

"The case had a motion sensor which apparently telephoned the device or devices which detonated in the gas towers at the refinery. The explosion was massive. The TV doesn't do it justice. The Feds are on their way and our office needs to liaise with them, sir. We need to be careful. With the technology they are using, first detonator may well trigger a second, so any attempt to open the case and see the mechanism could trigger a second explosion. We don't know. We need to alert all the PDs not to touch the cases until we have figured out how they work. Has our friend said anything?"

"No."

"Son of a bitch. Why? What about your man from—"

"Don't say it. He hasn't arrived yet. There are surprisingly few people willing to undertake that kind of job, even in specialized agencies."

"Are you sure? Take a drive around Jersey or the Bronx, I think you'll find a few who are willing. You won't even have to pay them. They'll do it for the fun."

"You jest, but I may well have to do that. We are running out of time, Alex."

"Sir, we need to cut corners here. The Mafia do this kind of stuff routinely. Anyhow, the good news is we have a guy here who may know something. Name is Jamil Abbad. I'll have the chief send you his DNA and his prints. You could check our databases. He's in surgery right now, but as soon as he comes out I'll be on him."

"Fine. Keep me posted."

I hung up and saw a uniform leaning in through the door.

"Mr. Mason?"

"Yeah."

"Sir, there's a lady downstairs says she has information, but will only speak to you."

ELEVEN

I MADE MY WAY TOWARD THE STAIRS WITH THE uniform at my shoulder.

"You told her I was here?"

"No sir. She came in asking for you."

I stopped at the top of the stairs and looked him in the eye. "So how'd she know I was here?"

He was very blond and his cheeks went red. "I don't know, sir. She came in real excited and upset, asking for Alex Mason. She said she had information. I tried talking to her but she was real insistent. She wouldn't talk to nobody unless it was Alex Mason."

"OK."

I trotted down the stairs and saw her immediately. She was leaning against the reception desk in a gray mac crying. She had blonde hair, blue jeans and white sneakers. As soon as she saw me she moved toward me. Her voice was on the edge of shrill.

"Are you Alex Mason?"

"Yes. Who are you?"

"I'm *Claire!*" She said it with a small stamp of her foot. Like she'd told me a hundred times already. "Claire *Wilson!* I'm Chet's *girlfriend.* Is it true he's *dead?*"

She had a strange cadence to her voice that reminded me of Christopher *Wal*ken. I ignored her question and asked one of my own.

"How'd you know I was here?"

"*Chet!*" she said, with that same "I told you a thousand times" tone, and I told myself if she kept it up I was going to put her across my knee. Instead I nodded and took hold of her arms. "You got a car?"

She nodded. "Uh-huh."

"Give me the key." I turned to pink cheeks and told him, "Tell Macdonald I'm at the hospital. I'll call him."

Outside she had a beaten-up Ford pickup. She gave me the key and I climbed behind the wheel. She got in the passenger seat and I pulled out of the parking lot and onto the I-20, west. The light had an ugly, dirty gray quality to it because of the vast, black cloud that now filled the entire southeastern sky behind us. The few cars that were on the road had their headlamps on.

"So let's start again," I said, "and quit whining and stamping your foot like you were four. I'm Alex Mason, you are Claire Wilson, Chet Baker's girl. Now, explain to me, one, how did he know about me? Two, why did he talk to you about me? And three, what have you got to tell me?"

She studied me with a pouting mouth and resentful eyes. "You're not a very nice man."

"Cut it out! Answer the questions."

I accelerated hard and almost hit a hundred before I had

to brake and come off onto South Garfield. It was two miles through town from there to the Midland Memorial Hospital, and we did it in less than two minutes. She didn't talk all the way there. When I pulled into the parking lot, the wind had changed and the sky was turning black overhead. I killed the engine and turned to face her.

"You came looking for me because you wanted to talk to me. Here I am. We have exactly zero time to waste. Now let me explain this to you. Right now you have two options: one, die in a nuclear blast; two, spend the rest of your life in a high-security prison under the Patriot Act. Your third option is quit acting like you're daddy's little girl, which is really pissing me off, get real and tell me what information you have."

She became serious, wiped her cheeks with her fingers instead of her palms, and licked the tears from her lips.

"Is it true Chet is dead?"

"Yes. I'm sorry."

She nodded. "I told him he was reckless and it was dangerous, but he never listened to anybody. Will you buy me a coffee? I drove all the way from San Francisco."

I jerked my head toward the hospital. "Let's go inside."

At the reception desk I showed the girl my card and told her, "The second Jamil Abbad is awake you call me. I'll be in the cafeteria. Before you call the Midland PD, before you tell the Bureau, before you do anything else, you tell me."

She blinked at me several times. "Sir, I don't know..."

I was shaking my head. "No, that is the wrong answer. You see this card? It means when you talk to me it's as though you were talking to the president. I'll be having coffee. And the instant you hear that he can talk, you call me."

She nodded. "Yes sir."

We found the Market Café in the hospital and I ordered two coffees and a couple of chicken and salad baguettes. The kid behind the counter asked me from on high whether I would prefer a vegan alternative. I told him I didn't approve of eating vegans, even as an alternative. He didn't laugh. He'd heard them all before.

As I handed him my money I told him, "Don't be an agelast. Life's too short."

He gave the smile of one who has scored a vegan point. "One of the benefits of the vegan diet, sir. One ages more slowly."

I surrendered, defeated by a relentlessly woke vegan with no vocabulary beyond "look at me," and carried my tray to the table where Claire was waiting, pulling at the cuffs of her jacket. I handed her her baguette and her coffee and said, "Talk."

"Do you have to be so brutal all the time? I just lost my boyfriend."

"Do you watch the news? We're on the clock."

She eyed me a moment. "Will I get arrested?"

"No. Keep stalling and there won't be anybody to arrest you."

She sighed. "Me and Chet are from Frisco."

I bit into my chicken roll and spoke with my mouth full. "Frisco?"

"Yeah." She frowned. "You know, San Francisco?" I nodded. She went on. "So Chet was a small-time dealer, weed and stuff. And this British guy—" She paused like something was making her uncomfortable. "Actually, you know? I always imagine British guys like, white? But this guy was like an Arab." She pronounced it Ay-rab. "He said his name was Jamil? And he wanted Chet to do a job for him."

"What kind of job?"

"Like he wanted him to deliver some dope or something—"

"What was it, dope or something?"

"I don't know. I think he said it was dope. Jamil would book him into a hotel, and all he had to do was show up with a couple of suitcases, check into the room, leave the cases there in the wardrobe and leave. That was it, and for that he was gonna pay him ten grand plus expenses. He had to pick up a suitcase in Los Angeles and take it on a Greyhound to Midland, Texas. I told him." She paused, shaking her head. "I told him, don't do it. If you're selling dope, you don't do it like that. Nobody does that. You know what I mean? That ain't how you do it."

"You made your point, Claire. It was not a typical dope deal. So what happened?"

"Well, it was easy money. Or that was what *Chet* thought. And Chet would do anything for easy money. Anyhow, as the date got closer he started getting more nervous. He said he didn't like the way it was goin' down. He said it didn't *feel* like a dope deal, which was what I was tellin' him all along. And he didn't like the fact that this British guy was, like, an Arab. Chet could be kind of racist."

"OK, Claire, now I want you to explain to me, clearly and precisely, how he came across my name."

"Well, I don't know. He come home one day, four or five days before he was coming here on the bus, and he told me he was worried, and if anything went wrong I should find Alex Mason. He said he would call me as soon as he had dropped the cases at the hotel, and as soon as he got paid he'd come straight home. But he never did call and he never come home. And next thing I see this huge explosion in Midland and I come rushin' here in my car as fast as I could. I ain't hardly slept in twenty-four hours."

I considered her for a moment. Her accent seemed to be drifting from Southern California to the Dakotas by way of Texas and South Carolina. About the only place she didn't sound like she was from was San Francisco.

"Where are you from, Claire?"

"I told you, I'm from Frisco."

"So when Chet told you to contact me, what did you say?"

She looked blank. "I told him OK."

"You didn't ask him who I was?"

"Oh, sure, I said, 'Well who the hell is Alex Mason?'"

"And what did he say? Try to be very precise, Claire. This is very important."

"Um, um…" Her eyes traced a line across the ceiling. "Well, he said he had called the Midland PD and he had talked to…" She trailed off, staring at her coffee. "Chief Hanratty?" I nodded. She went on, "Who had told him to talk to Detective…Macdonald, I remember because it was like the hamburger." She simpered, then became serious. "Sorry. That's inappropriate. So Macdonald told him that if he had anything more than a hunch, he should call you. But so far he was just moving a suitcase. I remember he said he told him, 'If you're suspicious, look inside. I ain't got time to waste.' And that's when he said if he had anything more than a hunch he should call you."

I nodded and sat stirring my coffee and thinking. She said, "Can I go to the john?"

I nodded without looking at her. "Sure."

While she was gone I turned the story over in my head, trying to organize all the holes in it and trying to make sense of the whole thing. There were too many aspects of it that just didn't ring true. For a start I never yet met anyone from San Francisco who called the city Frisco. Most of them would turn their nose up at you for doing so. Equally, if she was from San Francisco, why did she keep slipping into a hybrid Texas-cum-Arizona drawl with notes of the Carolinas, Tennessee and Wyoming? And then there was the fact that she had Chet talking to the chief and Macdonald at a time when he was probably already dead. While I thought I called Macdonald.

"Yup."

"Think carefully. Did you get a call a couple of days ago from a guy who was worried because he was being asked to shift a couple of suitcases from San Francisco to Midland? It would have been forwarded to you by Chief Hanratty, and you told this guy to call me."

There was a moment's silence, then, "Does that sound likely to you? I mean, aside from the timing which is just plain wrong."

"Not very, but there was a lot of heavy stuff going down and nobody has time for timewasters, right? Think about it, Seth. It's important. He told you he didn't feel comfortable about the suitcases and you told him if he wasn't sure what was in them to open them and have a look."

He was quiet for a moment, then said, "No." And then, "No, no, who's tellin' you this?"

"Chet Baker's girlfriend. I asked her why she was asking for me and how she knew my name. She said Chet called Hanratty before he brought the cases here, or maybe just after, because he was uncomfortable about the whole deal. He told her Hanratty put him onto you and you told him to look in the cases if he wasn't sure, and if he had anything more than a hunch, to call me."

"That makes me look real bad."

"No, it makes you look like a cop who was under too much pressure to listen to the paranoid bellyaching of some kid who has no evidence to offer. Come on, Seth, the suitcases have been all over Facebook, Twitter and Instagram, as well as the television, the radio and the papers. Now some kid calls saying somebody asked him to shift a couple of cases from San Francisco to Midland by Greyhound bus. What are you going to tell him? If you don't know what's in the damned case, open it and have a look! And then, quite properly, you told him if he had something more than a hunch, to call me."

I made it sound as reasonable as I could and he listened to the whole thing in silence. When I'd finished he said, "Ten out of ten for delivery. Nobody called me and I didn't tell anyone to call you. Besides, I had never heard of you till after Chet Baker was dead. Satisfied?"

"Of course. No offense, Macdonald."

"Oh, now I ain't Seth anymore? None taken. You'd better call the chief before I do."

Claire reappeared and sat while Hanratty's phone was ringing.

"Yeah, Hanratty."

"Chief, it's Mason here. Did you take a call a couple of days back from a man who said he'd been told to bring two suitcases from San Francisco to Midland? He said he was uncomfortable about it. You passed him on to Macdonald." He sighed noisily so I added, "It's important, Chief."

"Yeah, I am sure it is, but I have no idea. You know how many calls I get each day? There's a hundred and forty thousand people in this town, and they all think I am gonna solve their problems for them. Mrs. Jensen's cat is stuck up a tree, Mrs. Brown's Bobby is smoking dope when he was always such a good boy, Mr. Petersen's neighbors play their music too loud." It was my turn to sigh, loudly. "Oh, I'm sorry," there was bile in his voice, "am I boring you?"

"Yes. Did you get the call, Chief, or not?"

"I told you, I have no idea."

"Do you at least remember passing a call on to Macdonald?"

"Yeah, but not one, more like fifty. If I get a hundred calls I take maybe two or three. The rest I pass on to my detectives or other staff. That's what they are there for. Now can I ask you why you are wasting your goddamn time on this BS instead of finding out who bombed our oil refinery?"

"No. You can't. And Chief, next time I ask you a question you had better be ready to answer it, or I'll have you directing traffic in Lajitas at five bucks an hour before your leather swivel chair has had time to cool down from all the use you give it with your ass."

I hung up and Claire gave me a sheepish smile.

"I guess you don't believe me, huh?"

I shook my head once. "Nope."

"Everything I said is true."

"You're not from San Francisco." She sighed and looked away and her cheeks colored. "And don't tell me you're from Arizona, Idaho or Montana. Your Western y'all accent is as fake as your 'Frisco.' Genuine San Franciscans are very sensitive about anyone calling their beautiful city Frisco or San Fran. It is San Francisco, epicenter of the Summer of Love. And I'll tell you something else, I don't think there is an American alive who doesn't know that."

"Wow, and I thought I was doing so well." She pronounced her "I" as "oi" and her "well" as "will."

"You're a Kiwi."

"Yis," she said, exaggerating it a little. "You're pretty smart."

"My department only employs pretty smart people. So, do we have to go back to the beginning and do it all again? Do I have to remind you, Claire, that there are hundreds of thousands of lives at stake here? Or maybe you don't care. Maybe you're involved in placing the cases."

Her eyes widened in alarm. "*No!*"

"Let me assure you of something." I leaned forward with my elbows on the table. "I'm a nice guy, on the surface, but underneath I am a really nasty son of a bitch. And if I get the slightest notion that you are involved in this business, I will arrest you under the Patriot Act, whisk you off to a remote location and do things to you that will make waterboarding sound like a fun game at Water World." She went pale and I enunciated. "We have no time for bullshit."

Tears started in her eyes. "I'm sorry. Everything I've told you is the truth. I just have this really stupid habit, Chet was always complaining about it. I just try to pretend I'm American to see if I can get away with it. But we *did* live in San Francisco, and everything else is true. I swear!"

I grunted, feeling I was going around in circles and nothing much made sense.

"This guy Chet was in touch with. You said his name was Jamil?"

"Yes."

"Surname?"

"I don't know, but he was British."

"Did you ever see him? Did he ever come to your house? Were you ever introduced?"

She nodded, then shook her head vigorously. "Once. I saw him once. It was strictly him and Chet, always. But this one time we were in a car park—a parking lot—and Chet went over to talk to him. I wasn't supposed to be there but I kind of hunkered down in the seat and watched. Chet was always taking risks."

"Would you recognize him if you saw him again?"

"Yeah, I'm pretty sure I would."

"OK." I stood. "Let's go see if he's awake."

Her eyebrows shot up. "You mean he's here? That bastard who killed Chet is here in the hospital?"

I gave my head a small twitch. "Let's go find out."

She stared at me for a long moment, then stood.

TWELVE

Maria drove slowly, but before they had gone a mile, when they were close to the woods they had seen on the way to the town, she stopped the car and started to weep. José sighed. "Don't cry," he said. "You know I can't bear it when you cry."

She took a handkerchief from her purse and blew her nose. "I wanted so much for this to be wonderful for us. I have been so stupid. I imagined introducing you to my old family. They would be so proud I had married a civil servant."

He hunched his shoulders and spread his hands. It was a very Latin gesture.

"How can you introduce me to your family if you lie to me about everything?"

She looked at him and started crying again. "I know, I have been so stupid. Please forgive me, José. I have ruined everything. Will you let me try to fix it?"

He spoke quietly, taking her hand. "Of course."

"I told you my uncle was senile, he has Alzheimer's, so we can't go in. He panics. He doesn't understand. But can I call my cousin to come, with his wife, and I introduce you?"

He looked around him at the growing dark. "Here?"

"It will just be five minutes, to shake hands and you can thank them for the cheese and the ham."

He sighed and shrugged. "OK, call them. But isn't it easier if we go back and they come out...?"

But she was already dialing. She waited a moment and smiled at him, then started speaking in Russian. After a couple of minutes she hung up, leaned forward and kissed him. "I love you so much, José. These years being married to you have been the happiest of my life."

She kissed him again, for a long time, until they both heard the car pull up beside them. They heard the two doors slam and she gave him another kiss on the lips. "Come on," she said. "Let's get out and I'll introduce you."

He fixed a smile on his face and, as she climbed out of the driver's side, so he climbed out too and looked across the roof of the Audi. There he saw a large, swarthy man who was not smiling. He had his arm extended across the roof and at first José thought he wanted to shake his hand. But then he saw the glint of metal. He realized it was a gun and, as everything began to make some bizarre kind of sense, a small part of his brain told him it wasn't possible, because that this sort of thing didn't happen to him. Then he looked at Maria's face and saw that it was impassive, devoid of feeling. There was no remorse there, no love, only indifference.

Then reality exploded and he ceased to exist.

Dimitri, the man who had shot him through the head, and Jelko, who had remained in the background, carried the body into the woods and buried it. Meanwhile Maria made another telephone call. Colonel Alexandrina Vitsin answered on the second ring.

"Why are you calling?"

"José became suspicious. I had to kill him."

"You killed him yourself?"

"No, Dimitri did it. He and Jelcko are burying him now in the forest."

"You are not in Poland?"

"No, Orepichi."

"You need a husband."

"I know."

"This changes things. I need to think...

"I am sorry, Colonel. I had no choice."

She ignored the apology. "Peter is going to the United States. I will tell him to meet you in Croatia."

"Peter Belov?"

"Yes. You know each other."

"From many years ago. I went to Spain. He went to England."

"Is it a problem?"

"No, Colonel. Not at all. All I want is to do my job to the best of my ability. I am sorry I have caused an inconvenience."

"Don't worry, *zaychik*[1], you did the right thing. I will work out an itinerary. You have the case. That is the important thing."

"Yes, Colonel."

There was an unpleasant smile in the colonel's voice when she answered.

"Everybody is crazy searching for that case in United

States. They do not realize..." She was overcome with halting laughter that sounded more like a racking smoker's cough. "They don't realize, it is in *Belarus!*"

Maria smiled. "Yes, Colonel. It is wonderful."

"Good, good, *zaychik*, go. You have long drive ahead of you to Croatia. Six or seven hundred miles. You should make it in eight hours if you do not sleep. Peter will have papers for you."

It was seven hundred miles as the crow flies. As the road weaves it was more like fourteen hundred and took her close to fifteen hours, driving through the night, frequently breaking the speed limit, and stopping only twice for coffee and chocolate to keep her awake.

She crossed four countries on her way. From Poland to the Czech Republic, then Austria, where she really put her foot down, and Slovenia. All were part of the European Union, and all waved her Spanish-registered car through without interest or curiosity.

Finally, at ten AM the next morning, exhausted and with a splitting headache, she cruised through Dragonja, on the Croat-Slovenian border. There was no border post. She simply exited the small town, turned right and was in Croatia. She had arrived.

She lifted her sunglasses onto her head and wiped her eyes, and was surprised to discover she was crying. She reached for a handkerchief in her purse and dried the tears, glancing at herself in the mirror as she went. It would not be good for Peter to see her showing emotion. She gave a small snort. She did not *feel* any emotion, so why on Earth should she show it? She had long been aware that her organic being produced all the physical expressions of emotion, while she herself felt nothing. It was a paradox.

It was true that since Vienna she had found it difficult to remove the memory of José from her head. She had tried several techniques she had learned over the years, but hard as she had tried, he kept coming back in vivid color; and his voice too, clear, loud and precise. She assumed it was because they had been to Vienna on their honeymoon. He had been obsessed with Mozart, and the Strausses. It had been fun. For a little while it had been almost like being normal. They had gone to concerts, and eaten obscene cakes with wonderful coffee, and they had stayed at a five-star hotel. Her first five-star hotel.

She had remembered all that vividly as she skirted the city on the A23, and she had smiled. And then she had seen in her exhausted mind how José frowned at the Sig Sauer in Dimitri's hand. How he had turned to her, seeking an answer; seeking answers; seeking to understand how she could do what she had done.

She did not try to justify what she had done. That was for others to do, judges and psychologists. For her, moral justification was a fool's game. You did what you had to do. Then you found ways, strategies for dealing with it. There were techniques. She knew because she had studied them. The best one she had found was to turn the memory black and white, freeze the action, push the frozen, black and white image far away, notice the feeling of peace...

But she was too tired. The trip had more demanding than she had expected. The fourteen-hour drive had drained her of mental strength. She saw ahead on her right a service station and pulled in and parked intending to have some coffee and rest for a few minutes. But as she killed the engine she was engulfed by an attack of convulsive sobbing. She had the strange sensation of being outside of herself observing her body hunched over the steering wheel. More than sobbing she seemed to be retching, vomiting. It was an organic, visceral purging. She heard herself cry out, watched herself clutch at her belly and her mouth as she uttered inarticulate, ugly noises. She watched and told herself it would soon pass. It was like being sick. It would pass.

She told herself she needed coffee to wake herself up, Peter would be waiting, she should not delay. But the spasms would not stop, and every time they seemed to subside into sobbing, José's betrayed eyes would look at her over the roof of the Audi in the darkness, and the convulsions would start again.

She reasoned that it could not go on indefinitely. At some point it had to stop. Clearly that night she would be dining with Peter, and she could not do so convulsing in tears. He had to tell her their travel arrangements and she was already late.

In the end it took some ten minutes, almost a quarter of an hour. As her breathing slowed and steadied she remembered nights of crying alone when she was a child, and the peace she felt as her convulsions subsided. That peace was a comfort. She did not find that comfort in anybody else. No one had come then to hug her and soothe her. She had found her peace by herself, in herself.

She sat a while. The feeling of detachment gone. She blew her nose and dried her eyes, allowed the image of José's questioning face once more into her mind, but this time she drained it of color and action. She saw it as an old, black and white newspaper photograph. Then she pushed it away, making it smaller and smaller, aware of the calm, cold peace she felt in her heart, until he winked out of existence.

She did it a couple more times, until she got bored, then she climbed out of the car and called Peter as she crossed the parking lot toward the café.

His voice was smooth, elegant and unruffled, as it always had been.

"Darling, where are you? I am impatient to see you."

He spoke in flawless, cut-glass English and she answered in English almost as good as his, but she had an accent. She laughed. "Did they tell you it was a seven-hour drive too? It was fifteen and I am *exhausted!* I have crossed four or five countries to get to you. I hope you feel flattered."

"I am glowing, but where are you?"

"I am three miles inside the Croatian border, darling, southwest of Dragonja, on the E751. I *need* a coffee!"

He gave a small, indulgent laugh. "Of course you do, my darling. Why don't you sit and have breakfast and I come and get you?"

"That would be lovely, but what about my car, and my cases?"

"We'll put your cases in my trunk, and we'll have someone come and collect your car."

"Oh, darling," she said, as the doors slid back to allow her access to the café, "that sounds perfect. I am *so* tired, you can't imagine."

He was quiet for a moment, then said, "Alexandrina told me everything. I can imagine, Maria."

"OK, my love! I'll see you in about an hour!"

She hung up, got herself a large coffee with plenty of sugar and cream, and two chocolate croissants. Then she sat by the large, plate-glass window where she could watch for Peter's arrival.

It took him fifty minutes, by which time she had had a second breakfast. She did not wait for him to come to the café. She exited the automatic doors and trotted across the parking lot to meet him as he climbed out of his Jaguar. They made a big show of being husband and wife, separated for an interminable few days. They hugged and kissed, and she was aware that the feeling was therapeutic. Perhaps she was getting old. Perhaps it was time to start thinking about early retirement.

He had recognized the Audi and parked next to it, and now removed her cases from the trunk and transferred them to the Jag.

"We were going to take a cruise from Pula to New York," he told her, "but we are starting to run behind schedule, and events in the States are not going exactly to plan." They climbed into the Jag and he pulled out of the service station lot, headed south toward Pula, among dense woodlands and lush, green fields, under a perfect Mediterranean sky.

What's happened?" she asked, fingering strands of hair from her face.

"One of the agents went AWOL, and as a result the Texas bomb was triggered a little ahead of what we had wanted. I imagine you've not been following the news. It has impacted the stock market, but not as severely as we had hoped. There is now a massive hunt for the bomb and, from what we can tell from our sources, the hunt is focused on Washington DC, as we had hoped."

She nodded. "That's good."

"Yes, it is good, but the pressure is on us to get the suitcase in place before the penny drops."

"Yes, so?"

"So, we have chartered a plane to Bermuda. In Bermuda we pick up a cruise for New York, which will arrive in Manhattan the day after tomorrow." He glanced at her. "It was nearly cancelled, with the suitcase crisis, which would have been a problem, but the White House is falling over itself trying to reassure everyone this is all just a hoax, and that the Texas explosion was simply an industrial accident." He paused, watching the road. "Ideally we would go into phase two now and prove that it is not all a hoax, but before we can do that, we must get to New York. So you see, we are a little out of step."

"Why don't we just fly to New York?"

"The colonel believes that airport security will be tighter, especially on private and chartered planes, than coming off a cruise ship. She may be right."

She glanced at him. It was a naked display of arrogance to say that Colonel Alexandrina Vitsin "*might* be right." There could be no question or doubt about that. She was *always* right. But it was typical of Peter to make that kind of comment. One day, she was sure, it would cost him his career, if not his life.

"Of course she is right," she said quietly.

"Of course," he said, and smiled. Then he compounded his lack of respect by saying, "You were one of her special projects, weren't you? You believe she is infallible."

She looked away. "She is the best. I have never known her to fail."

He gazed at her a moment, still smiling. "You can rest on the plane," he said. "It's an eight-hour flight."

"I need it."

For a horrific moment she thought he was going to ask her about José. But he was too experienced, to much of a professional for that. Instead his smile shifted indefinably, his eyes became hooded and conspiratorial and he allowed them to rove over her body.

"We will be husband and wife for the next week or two. We need to be convincing. We need to become intimate. You understand that. This is like method acting."

She smiled back. "Keep your eyes on the road, Peter. All we need now is for you to crash the car because you are gaping at my legs and my tits."

She started to laugh and he laughed too. "Can you imagine?" he said. "Croatia wiped from the map of Europe because of aroused driver!"

She half-squealed with laughter and became helpless, almost hysterical. "*Biggest orgasm in history!*" she gasped.

They laughed some more, he in control, she curled up against the door and covering her face with her hands. Then she wiped the tears from her eyes and took hold of his hand. She had a strange, secret smile on her face. "It will be good," she said. "I need it." He glanced at her and nodded. "Be rough," she added. "Punish me. I have been bad, Peter. I have been very bad," and she started to cry.

"I know," he said, and there was an unexpected compassion in his voice. He did know. He had been there and he had done it, and he didn't need to tell her so. "I know, Maria."

THIRTEEN

Dr. Jackson Wong had his eyes closed behind his bottle base glasses and very carefully and deliberately interrupted me, repeatedly, every time I tried to speak.

"I fully appreciate who you are and why you are here, Mr. Mason, but *my patient* is in recovery after emergency surgery and *he-cannot-be-interrogated*. And that is *final*."

It was the third time he had cut across me and talked me down with the same words and I knew if he did it a third time I was going to stick his head down the can and flush it. So I said, "Dr. Wong. Will you please stop talking? I need you to be silent and listen to me. If you interrupt me one more time I am going to clap you in irons and take you to Virginia for extended interrogation. Do you understand me?"

His cheeks colored and his eyes filled with tears of righteous anger. "I think I had better call my lawyer."

He went to walk away and I said, "One." He turned and frowned at me. I said, "Just take one step." And there must have been something in the way I said it that made him pause.

"Now you listen to me. *I-do not-want-to-talk-to-your-patient.*" I raised a finger. "Don't even dream about interrupting me." I could see the muscles going on his jaw. "You are going to show me where he is, so that this young lady can identify him. And you are going to do it without talking."

"This is *intolerable!*"

"Indeed. Lead on."

He gathered his dignity about him and strode down the corridor, his white coat flapping, muttering about the police state and basic liberties. We came to a door, he opened it and went through. Claire and I followed after him, but all I could see from where I stood in the doorway was the back and side of her blonde head. She was staring at something out of my line of vision, and I saw the doctor frown. She said, "Oh, yes. That's him all right." And the doctor moved toward the bed.

My heart gave a single, powerful thud and I pushed past her. I saw Dr. Wong leaning over a form lying in the bed. I could see one dark hand, and my eyes took in several monitors ranged beside his bed. I noticed they were silent, then realized they were all switched off. Dr. Wong turned and stared at me.

"He's dead."

He said it in that "told you so" voice, like it was my fault his patient was dead. I felt a rush of anger in my belly but suppressed it.

"How?" I snapped.

"I *beg* your pardon?"

"*How was he killed? God damn it!*"

"I can't possibly know that until we've done an—"

I grabbed him by the scruff of his neck, dragged him across the floor and shoved him out of the room. "Get out! Stay out!"

Then I grabbed my cell from my pocket, called Macdonald, put it on speaker and handed it to Claire. "Hold that and stand close."

She did both. It rang twice and Macdonald's voice said, "You again?"

"Jamil is dead."

"*What?* You have got to be kidding me! How?"

"I am looking now, but it looks pretty clear to me. He was stabbed through the heart, with a fine blade."

"What is this, some kind of gang thing?"

"A gang with access to thermobaric bombs and nuclear devices? That's some gang."

"Every God-darned one of 'em with a knife."

"It is still the most efficient and discreet way of killing someone. And these people are all about discretion and efficiency. I need you here, now. I need the ME and I need a crime scene team. And I need uniforms talking to *everyone*. Somebody came into this room and stuck a knife in this guy's heart in the last fifteen minutes. We need that person and we need them *now!*"

He'd already hung up by the time I'd finished. I took back the phone, propelled Claire out of the room and used my handkerchief to close the door. Claire muttered, "I think you've got trouble."

I looked up and saw Wong descending on me with two private security bad boys. I pulled my card from my wallet again and held it up as they approached. I showed it to the least simian looking of the two apes.

"You know what this is?" He frowned. I said, "Read it. It says, Office of the Director of Intelligence Networks, and here it says, 'Pentagon.'" They both looked impressed. "You watch the news?" They nodded. "You seen the sky lately? It's black, right?" They nodded again. "Good, you're still with me. Now, you," I pointed to the more simian of the two, "get this clown to a patient who needs him and make sure he stays out of my way. And you, you stay here on this door and you do not let anyone in until the cops get here. And the cops means Detective Macdonald, so you look at his badge. Understood?"

"Yes, sir!"

He saluted smartly and planted himself in front of the door like a Marine. To Claire I said, "Come with me."

We went out to the parking lot and I called Nero. When he answered he sounded depressed.

"Our man has just arrived. We are about to go down."

"Jamil was murdered."

He sighed heavily. "We have reports of murders now from Alamogordo, Los Angeles and San Francisco Bay Area. They all follow the same modus operandi. We are losing our grip on the situation."

"I thought the same thing a while back. Then I realized we never had a grip on the situation in the first place, sir. And that made me feel better. They have been five steps ahead all the way."

"Everything depends on making the general speak, then."

"I'm coming back to DC."

"Yes, there's nothing much you can do there."

I hung up and Claire said, "What about me?"

"What about you?"

"What am I going to do?"

I was about to tell her to go back to San Francisco, but stopped. "If you're smart you'll go back to New Zealand. Failing that, stay away from Texas, Los Angeles, San Francisco, Washington DC and New York."

"That doesn't leave much!"

"I haven't time to talk, Claire. Take me to the airport, will you?"

"Sure, nice."

I called the pilot. "I'll be there in ten minutes. We're going back to DC." He acknowledged the order and I hung up. We climbed into her truck and I called Macdonald again while she reversed and pulled out.

"Sweet mother of God! What now?"

"I'm going back to DC."

"Good!"

"I need whoever killed Jamil, Macdonald. Talk to the governor. Impose martial law if you have to. I don't think you appreciate—"

"Don't say it, Mason. This is my town. Just have a look at the sky and tell me I don't appreciate. Now get the hell out of here and let me do my job!"

I hung up and we headed for the airport under a black sky. Claire was silent as she drove until we were halfway there. Then she said, "Take me with you."

I frowned at her. I may have scowled at her. "What?"

"Take me to DC with you."

"Why the hell would I do that?"

"I may be able to help you?"

"How?"

She took a deep breath and held it, then burst out, "No, see? You're clever and you're going to try and get everything out of me and then you won't take me with you!"

"Claire, what is this 'everything' I am going to get out of you? We are facing the threat of a nuclear explosion of unknown magnitude. We cannot be playing games. If you have information you have to give it to me."

"See?" she said, and thumped the steering wheel. "You're doing it already. Now you're making me feel guilty."

"Jesus!" I stared at the ceiling of the car and counted to ten. "Give me patience. Do you know something about DC or not?"

"I'm not sure. Chet said some things. I didn't pay much attention. But I think if I was there, and saw the streets and stuff, I might remember."

We had arrived at the airport. She pulled in and parked and we sat staring at each other. Finally I asked her, "What's in DC?"

"It's not so much what's in DC. It's what's back in Fris—in San Francisco. Chet owed money. Now he's gone, I owe money. Give me a ride to DC and I can start over."

"Do you have any information, Claire? I keep repeating this but no one seems to get it. *Hundreds of thousands of lives* could be at risk, men, women, children..."

"OK! OK... Yes, Chet did say some things. But I am feeling really stressed right now. I am serious. Let me come with you, talk to me." She stared right into my eyes and there was something childlike and compelling about her face. When she spoke it was in a breathless rush. "You're good at asking questions. I think if we talk on the plane, and you ask me questions, you could probably get stuff I don't even know I know! I know he mentioned DC and he mentioned streets and stuff—"

"Claire." She stopped. "This is not a game!"

"I know that!"

"I cannot spend hours talking to you while these bastards set off one explosion after another and shut down the American economy!"

"So get a hypnotist to regress me. I know I know something. I remember him talking about DC. It *will* come to me if you stop being such a jackass!"

"Fine." I took a deep breath and nodded. She was, after all, right. This was Chet's girlfriend and as good a lead as any other. It would be foolish not to explore it to the end. "I'll take you to DC. I'll debrief you on the plane."

"Debrief!" She snapped her fingers. "You get trained in that shit, right?"

"And we'll help you get settled once this is over."

"Cool."

We locked the truck and started toward the tarmac. I stopped and stared at her. "You haven't got a bag? A toothbrush? A change of clothes?"

"No." She looked down at her white sneakers. "I left in a bit of a hurry. I didn't think."

"OK, come on. Let's get moving."

The Gulfstream was waiting with the steps down. A warm light spilled out into the deepening blackness and the high whine of the turbines filled the air. I saw the silhouette of the airhostess framed in the doorway and took Claire's elbow, and we ran the last few yards to the plane.

She was still closing the door as we took our seats and started to taxi toward takeoff. "Strap yourselves in," she said over her shoulder, "we'll be in the air in less than five minutes."

I watched Claire as we hurtled down the runway, lurched into the air and began to climb. Her eyes were wide and her cheeks were flushed. Her small hands were clutching the padded leather arms of her seat and she was staring around the cabin. She caught my eye and grinned.

"This is so *cool!*" I couldn't help laughing. Her grin deepened, like we were conspiring together. "You get to travel in private, luxury jets."

It wasn't a question. It was a statement of fact. "Sometimes," I said, "and never for pleasure."

"Right. It's always some kind of emergency. Wow, you're like this kind of James Bond, right?"

We had started to level off. I arched an eyebrow at her. "How old are you, Claire?"

She hesitated a little too long. "Twenty...five."

"Going on eighteen?"

"Come on! Don't patronize me. I *hate* being patronized."

"I'm not patronizing you. I'm going to have a martini. I want to know if you're old enough to join me."

"I'm twenty. I'll have a beer."

I told the hostess and she went to get them. "You were driving the truck back there like you'd been driving a long time. You got a driver's license? Any ID? You needed a passport to get here, right?"

"You want me to prove who I am?"

"Yup."

"I can't. Do I still get the drink?"

"Yeah, you get the drink. Why can't you show me any ID?"

"Because Jamil took it all. My papers and Chet's. He said he'd give them back when he paid him."

The hostess put a martini in front of me and a cold beer in front of Claire.

"How come you didn't mention this before?"

She nodded elaborately like I had made her point for her. "See? This kind of stuff is normal for you. But to me it's like the whole world has gone crazy. I saw what had happened, I grabbed my purse, stuffed it in my jeans and headed for Midland. All I could think was, Chet's dead and I have to find Alex Mason. Now, you tell me, when have I had a chance, before now, to actually sit down and think?"

I sipped. "In the cafeteria in the hospital."

She laughed out loud. "Are you kidding me? I was so tense you could have snapped me like a twig! I was convinced you were going to arrest me on the spot for conspiracy to murder, or terrorism, and lock me up for the rest of my life! And all *you* did to make me relax was threaten me!"

I stared at my ghost in the black porthole for a moment. Past my ghost, out in space, was Claire's ghost, staring at me.

"You hungry?"

"Famished."

I called the stewardess and she said she'd fix us some chicken sandwiches. While she was in the galley I asked Claire, "When did Chet first mention DC?"

She became abstracted, staring at the cockpit door. "About a week ago? I think Jamil hadn't made up his mind if he wanted Chet to go to Washington or Midland. I mean, I might be talking out of my arse, but that was the impression I got, looking back."

"Did he talk about any district in particular?"

"Yeah, it was an odd name like, like..." She thought for a moment. "Pen, Pencil? Does that make sense? Like a Pen?"

"Yes, but with two ns."

"The Penn area?"

"Quarter."

"OK, yeah, that's right." She nodded. That's it. The Penn Quarter."

"What about streets, landmarks?"

"Well, it's kind of confusing 'cause the streets in Washington are either numbers or letters, right?"

"Most of them, yeah."

"So he talked about...," she gave it some thought again, staring out the black window, "F Street? And G Street, maybe? Does any of this make sense?"

"Yeah, it makes sense. So what about F Street and G Street? What did he say about them?"

"So, maybe he said—" She faltered. "Look, I feel under a lot of pressure, OK? I know there is a hell of a lot riding on this. So please remember I'm dragging stuff up that I am not one hundred percent sure of."

"You're doing fine." I smiled to relax her. "So far you've earned your beer. What do you think he said about F Street and G Street?"

"Like, maybe he was going to stay in a hotel there?" She screwed up her face and almost winced. "I don't even know if there *is* a hotel there."

"What makes you think he was going to a hotel?"

She puffed out her cheeks. "Well, maybe I'm making it up." She glanced at me. "That's not sarcasm. I mean like, he stayed at a hotel in Midland. Maybe he was going to stay at a hotel in DC? But I'm pretty sure he said something about staying at a hotel and going to a fancy restaurant."

"Can you remember the name of the restaurant?"

She fiddled with her sleeves, chewing her lip. "That thing you Yanks call seafood and meat, sea and turf?"

"Surf and turf."

"Yeah, something like that." But her face said it wasn't quite right. "Prime? Prime steak and surf...nah! I'm making it up 'cause I can't remember."

"Don't worry. It's good enough. What about the hotel? An address? A name?"

"He said it was fancy, right by the White House. But in the end they sent him to Midland."

"Did he say why?"

She shrugged and shook her head. "Could it be the White House? Is there a hotel called the White House?" Before I could answer she said, "You know what would really help?" She put her head back and closed her eyes. "If we could drive around the area for a bit. I'm pretty sure the thing...it would..."

And she started snoring. Just like that.

FOURTEEN

I LET HER SLEEP. SHE HAD TOLD ME ENOUGH. WHAT was weighing on my mind more than Claire, as we flew over Arkansas and Kentucky, was the silence from Nero. He'd said he was bringing in a skilled interrogator. Any half-decent interrogator would have General Aleksandr Lebed singing like a nightingale within fifteen minutes, given the circumstances in which he was being held—without laying a finger on him. So why the silence?

I had two places I needed to be at the same time, and as much as Claire might end up being a help, right now she was a problem, not to mention a pain in my butt. We touched down at Ronald Reagan at eleven PM and I bundled Claire into a taxi and took her to my house. There I put her to bed in a guest room and locked her in. Then I trotted down the stairs to my car and sent Nero a message telling him I was on my way.

In theory it's a twenty-minute drive, but it was late, the roads were empty and I broke the speed limit all the way there, so I made it in fifteen. Lucas opened the door to me as I ran up the stoop, and actually spoke to me as he gestured toward the drawing room.

"In the drawing room, sir. He is expecting you."

He opened the door for me, I went in and he closed it behind me. I found Nero sitting like a giant, sulking dumpling in his triple-X chesterfield, staring at the cold grate.

"What the hell's going on?" I asked him. "Is your interrogator downstairs? We should have a result by now. What's taking so long..."

I trailed off because he wasn't even looking at me.

"I'm sorry, Alex. I can't do it."

"*What?*"

"It is the thing I most abhor. I have devoted my entire life to fighting it. I *detest* it. I understand it is all we have, but..."

He didn't finish. He closed his eyes. I spoke deliberately and quietly, repeating the litany. "Sir, we are talking about *hundreds of thousands of lives*, children..."

"I know. But I *can't!*"

"What about your interrogator?"

"He brought pliers, scalpels...I could not let him."

"Sir, precious hours, minutes, *seconds* are being lost!"

He turned on me, his huge face flushed and his eyes moist with rage. "*I cannot be responsible for torturing another human being! Don't you understand, Alex?*"

We stared at each other in silence for fifteen or twenty seconds, which is a long time to stare at someone. Finally I sighed and said, "Yes, I understand. If it's any consolation, I feel the same." I shrugged. "That's why I hightailed it out of here to Texas."

He frowned. I went and sat opposite him.

"Sir, I brought a girl back from Texas with me." His eyes went wide like I was insane. I ignored him and went on. "She was Chet's girlfriend and may have useful information on the DC suitcase."

"That's the one that counts."

"Exactly."

"That would be an enormous relief."

"Yes. She doesn't know if she knows, but she understands that by debriefing her with care, she might remember things. We might use a hypnotist, if we have time."

"If there's time, yes. I am quite a good hypnotist, Alex. Did you know that?"

"No, sir, I didn't. She's at my house, now, asleep in the guest room. I didn't want to leave her there alone, but I had no choice. Why don't..."

His face turned gray and he swallowed hard. Nero is the most honest man I have ever met, and it must have been hard for him to lie to himself, especially on that particular score. He said, "Why doesn't Lucas drive me over to your house, I can babysit the girl, perhaps debrief her, while you try to talk to the general again." He stared at me with wide eyes.

"I won't touch a hair on his head, sir. It takes a special kind of person to torture someone. I am not that kind of person."

He nodded, and there was gratitude in his gesture. "No, I don't believe you are."

"But I will be persuasive."

"Yes, we'll do that then." He levered himself out of the chair. "You will be humane…"

I nodded. "That's what we're all about, sir."

"Yes." He stopped and frowned at me. "Yes, Alex, it is what we are all about."

He left the room, calling Lucas, and five minutes later I watched them leave in the big, old Rolls Royce. Then I closed the door, went to the kitchen and found a large carving knife, a cleaver, a pair of pliers and a glazing torch. After that I went down to the cell, pulled on the balaclava and the latex gloves and opened the door. The fact was I didn't feel much like being humane, and I wasn't really sure how far I was prepared to go.

I found General Aleksandr Lebed sitting on the bed staring at the wall. As the door opened he turned to stare at me. I said:

"My boss is squeamish. But I have to be honest with you, General. If I put a few hours of your pain in the balance with the lives of a few hundred thousand people, maybe a hundred thousand kids, babies, mothers…" I trailed off and shook my head. "There is no contest. Especially as *you* have a choice. Save those lives and save yourself the hours of excruciating pain. Refuse to collaborate," I shrugged, "and go through hell. You will talk, and you will talk very quickly. So you may as well do it *before* I start removing things."

I waited. Nothing. I shrugged again.

"So I have sent my squeamish boss away. Now, I'm going to shoot you in the knee, partly so you can't get away, and partly so that you'll see I am serious. Then, bit by bit, I will dismember you." I showed him the cleaver and the knife, and the pliers. "And I will cauterize each wound, so you don't bleed to death. No way out. Not even death." I showed him the caramelizing torch. "I don't want to do this, General. This is not me. I don't approve of this stuff. But make no mistake that I will do it. And we have no time for playing games. So I am going to start by proving to you that I am serious."

He still didn't say anything, but he swallowed hard, which I guessed was progress. I pulled my P226 from under my arm, positioned myself six or seven feet from where he was sitting and aimed at his right knee. He said, "Wait!"

I said, "No, I'm sorry, General. I think I need to convince you I am serious."

His hands lifted as though to ward off the bullet. "No! You don't need to convince me. I only need to imagine myself in your position. I also would do anything that was necessary. If you start to cause me such extreme pain, I will become incoherent. Then you lose valuable time. I will talk. I will tell you what you need to know." He gestured at the gun and the knives. "You do not need to do this."

I didn't waver. "Prove it."

He gave a single nod.

"This comes direct from the Kremlin, from the president."

"That much we know." I pulled out my cell and started to record.

"That much you assumed. I am telling you. You have five dummy bombs. They are in suitcases and if you scan them— your FBI will scan them if they find them—they will not be able to distinguish, this one is real this one is dummy. The Texas case is dummy, but it has motion sensor trigger connected to powerful bomb placed against gas tower."

I drew breath but he raised a finger. "Now, I tell you, genuine nuclear device is here in DC. Primary blast area is three miles from epicenter. Epicenter is White House. So it erases White House, Capitol and Pentagon. Secondary, expansion wave, will devastate Virginia, Langley and Norfolk. All will be destroyed, and all the suburbs of Washington to the north and west."

"Where?"

He nodded again. "I am telling you. We are faster if you do not interrupt. In Los Angeles, Silicon Valley and New York there are dummies. But be careful because Los Angeles dummy will trigger bombs in Silicon Valley."

"OK, now answer straight and without prevarication, General. One, how do we neutralize the triggers, and two, *where is the DC bomb*?"

He sighed heavily. "To neutralize trigger you can do with powerful local EMP device. I know you have this. You put above case, trigger and it is neutralize. Then you can safely remove bombs from AI Solutions Incorporated, in Silicon Valley, also from MicroMedia International and Nano Global, NASA, Microsoft... But *first* neutralize case with EMP."

"OK." I sent the audio file to Nero with the message, "Take action on this, more coming." "So, first, where is the DC bomb, then where are the other bombs. *First* DC."

"Yes, first DC." He was staring me in the face and tears started to roll from his eyes. "Is many, many people die in DC. They must not die."

"This is not the time, General. Cut the theatrics, where is the DC bomb?"

"In hotel." He wiped his eyes with the back of his hand.

"In hotel, near White House..." He looked up at me and his bottom lip curled in on itself. I could see saliva on his chin and his cheeks were sodden with tears. His body began to shake with sobs. I got as far as, "What the hell...?" before the sobs turned into violent convulsions, he gripped his belly with both arms and let out a violent rasp. Foam began to spew from his mouth and he fell to the floor, thrashing violently.

I swore and dialed Nero.

"I have the—"

"I need a company doctor, *now!*"

"What have you done to him?"

"Nothing, goddamn it! He's taken poison!"

"Hang up and I'll call—"

"Forget it." He had become motionless. His eyes were bulging and he was staring fixedly at nothing two inches in front of his face. "He's dead."

"Did you get the name of the DC hotel?"

"No, but I think I know where it is. You'd better get the cleaners in to clean up the cell. I'm coming over to get Claire."

I ripped off the balaclava and the gloves, took the cleaver, the knife and my other instruments back to the kitchen. Then I got back in my car and drove at speed through the night back to my own house. The roads were desolate, eerie in the amber light of the lamps, like a vast, apocalyptic stage set. When I got there I saw the Rolls parked outside my front door. I parked behind it. My car door sounded loud in the night, and my feet on the stone stoop echoed in the empty street. Lucas opened the door to me and I went into the living room.

Nero was sitting beside the cold fireplace looking queasy, with a glass of my best whisky in his hand. Opposite him was Claire, looking sleepy, holding a cup of cocoa. I said to her, "Let's go."

"Where?"

"To F Street ad G Street."

"I don't know if..."

"You don't need to know if. You just need to get on your feet and get in the car."

She stared at me a moment, then nodded and said, "OK, can I put my shoes on?"

"Do it now. The seconds are ticking, Claire."

She went to the hall to pull on her sneakers and I turned to Nero.

"Sir, it may be time for you to think about leaving the capital."

He shook his head. "No."

"They will need you—minds like yours—afterwards."

"No. That is somebody else's problem. I don't want to be here afterwards. Just find the bomb, Alex. Find the bomb and defuse it."

"We are going to need an EMP device. If you can arrange one, you had better do it now and have it ready."

He nodded.

We ran down the steps and climbed in the Mk4. I drove fast down North Capitol Street, jumped the lights at an empty intersection and approached the White House at speed along New York Avenue. I slowed as we negotiated the Carnegie Library and then took the last half mile to 15th Street at an easy twenty miles an hour.

I paused at the intersection and she stared hard at the

Bank of America on her right, then across the road at the massive, neoclassical hulk of the Treasury, half concealed behind trees. There was no traffic, but I waited for the lights to change and eased onto 15th Street NW and moved slowly down past the treasury. I glanced at her and saw that her eyes were everywhere, wide with wonder. We passed G Street and she was sitting forward, staring hard at the buildings. We passed the Old Ebbid Grill and then F Street NW on our left. Then she sat up, eyes wide, pointing.

"That, there, I'm sure of it!" She turned to me, excited, bouncing in her seat. "You remember I told you! I told you it was something like the White House Hotel? This is it! The Washington!"

I pulled over, across the traffic if there had been any, and parked on the sidewalk under the awning, with my hazards flashing. The mahogany and brass doors opened and the porter, in an elaborate coat and a peaked cap, came out like a general in full regalia, smiling because it was an expensive car, but shaking his head.

"No, sir, I am sorry, you can't—"

I showed him my card. I was going to have to get a badge like the ones they had on TV. "Don't let anyone move it," I said. "Especially not the cops."

I pushed through the doors. Everything was quiet, dim and mahogany-and-brass. I approached the reception desk and showed the concierge my card. He looked French and sighed Frenchly, with arched eyebrows. I told him:

"Mr. Art Bernstein booked a room here..."

"Monsieur, I 'ave already been over zis wiz the detectives who came and ask me the same question..."

"I haven't asked you a question," I answered quietly,

suppressing the irritation and frustration that were building in my belly. He closed his mouth. I went on, "Don't interrupt me again or I will bring an army of uniformed cops and national guard here and I will sack the whole hotel. Now, which is Mr Bernstein's room?"

"Number seven fifteen, monsieur."

"Get the key and show me."

"I cannot do zat, monsieur."

"Why the hell not?"

"Because Monsieur Bernstein is lying down and 'as expressly asked *not* to be disturbed— *Monsieur!*"

I leaned across the counter and stared hard into his eyes. He gave me what in France probably passed for a "come at me, bro" look. I snarled, "Monsieur Art Bernstein is dead!"

"Not *zis* Monsieur Art Bernstein. Zis one is only sleeping!"

My mind was racing but didn't seem to be getting anywhere. In the end I said, "Get a key and take me to his room. If you don't, I will shoot you."

He looked more disdainful than scared, programmed a key and led the way to the mahogany and brass elevator that took us to the seventh floor. We emerged onto a thick, sage green carpet and he led the way down a corridor to a door with a "Do Not Disturb" sign hanging on the handle. He gestured to it. "Voila!" I pulled my P226 from under my arm. He rolled his eyes and muttered, "*Les américains! Toujours avec leurs flingues!*[1]"

I said, "Open the door."

He opened it. The room was dark. I gestured for him and Claire to move away, and stepped inside. The first door on the right was a bathroom. I peered inside. There was a toothbrush, some toothpaste, a disposable razor. The room had been occupied. I moved on into the bedroom. The heavy sage drapes were closed, but there was enough light from the open door behind me to make out the man lying on the bed. I turned back; the concierge and Claire were silhouetted in the doorway.

"Switch on the lights, will you?"

I holstered the Sig and as the lights came on I gestured at the bed. "Is this the man you know as Art Bernstein?"

For the first time he looked disconcerted. He approached, with Claire just behind him, and peered at the bed. He gasped and covered his mouth with his hand.

"I'm sorry. I need an answer. This one seems to be more dead than sleeping."

He nodded. I glanced at Claire. She was expressionless, staring fixedly at the corpse. He was stark naked, he was lying flat on his back and he had a kitchen knife stuck in his chest, left of center.

"Both of you, go stand by the door. Don't leave, don't let anybody in."

I used a handkerchief to open the wardrobe and saw an unopened, red Samsonite case. I pulled my cell from my pocket. He answered on the first ring.

"Have you found it?"

"I think so. We need our best man, or the Fed's best man. Whoever is the best. And sir, what the general said, before he left for the great borscht in the sky, was to use an EMP to disable it."

"You told me. It could be a trap. If he was willing to take his own life, he might also have given you the very instructions to detonate it."

I took a deep breath and sighed. He was right.

"In that case we should alert the president, sir, and evacuate the city."

"I'll alert him, and no doubt they'll make for Camp David, but neither he nor his advisers will allow the city to be evacuated. It will panic the stock market and cause pandemonium. In their view it will be as bad as detonating the bomb."

I closed my eyes. "But *they* will leave."

"Oh, yes. *They* will leave."

Behind me Claire said, "I think I know how to disarm it."

I turned and scowled at her. "*What?*"

"I think I know how to disarm the bomb."

FIFTEEN

PETER AND MARIA STEPPED DOWN FROM THE luxury Gulfstream G700 into the radiant sunshine of Bermuda's LF Wade International Airport. They were met by a buggy on the tarmac and a man in a peaked cap drove them to VIP customs. There an official nodded at their British passports without opening them and wished them an enjoyable stay in Bermuda. They collected his leather cases and her two red Samsonite cases and pushed their trolley out to the brilliant, near-Caribbean sunshine. There was a Bentley convertible waiting for them in the parking lot. Peter slung their cases in the spacious trunk and climbed behind the wheel. Maria got in beside him, leaned over and gave him a long, lingering kiss. They were newly married, and deeply in love.

"How long have we got, before the cruise departs?" she asked from behind her huge sunglasses under her straw hat.

He glanced at his watch. "About three and a half hours. We depart from King's Wharf, at the other end of Bermuda, at the Naval Dockyard. It'll take us twenty minutes or so to get there. We'll have just enough time to check our baggage on board and have a nice seafood lunch at the Bone Fish."

She raised her face and smiled up at the blue sky and the sun, reflected in her black lenses.

At the Royal Naval Dockyard she had the same position, in her chair on the terrace of the Bone Fish Bar and Grill. Looming massive behind her, gleaming white, was the vast form of the *Princess Diana*, less than two hundred yards away. While overhead, under the clear blue dome of the sky, the seagulls wheeled and cried havoc.

She sipped sparkling white wine and watched Peter, in his tropical white suit, with a burgundy cravat at his neck, stroll back toward her. She thought absently that he was the most extraordinary man she had ever met. It was as though he was devoid of doubt, and in having no doubt he was devoid of anxiety. He had only certainty. Yet certainty came in him as it appeared in a saint, peaceful, quiet, calm. She smiled and felt a stirring of desire she had never felt with any other man. He was calm, she thought, and ruthless. Utterly ruthless.

The exact opposite of José.

José had been a constant source of recrimination and criticism. He measured all people against his own unattainably anal standard. It was a standard which was too pathetically low to be measured, but which through the microscope of his own small mind he saw as perfect.

But Peter, unencumbered by morality, held nobody to any standard. He knew that where there was no good, there could be no standard. This was not a unique view, especially in Russia, but what made it unique in Peter was that it was not an intellectual posture. He was far beyond such under-graduate, Nietzschean dialectics. He knew viscerally, more than that, it was in the very fiber of his being. He knew it to such a level that it gave him peace, and he radiated that peace to all those about him. It was evil become goodness, yin become yang.

She smiled. With Peter she did not have to try or pretend. Peter liberated her, just by being Peter.

He returned her smile from behind black glasses, and sat, signaling the waiter.

"Peter," she asked him, "what will happen afterwards?"

He ordered oysters and more wine. When the waiter had gone he leaned back and crossed one long leg over the other.

"For my part I have been charged with buying assets in oil. That will probably be expanded to the fields of finance, banking. Prices will be at rock bottom."

She nodded. "There will be many in Congress who will be desperately searching for salvation in the form of a rich buyer."

He gave a small laugh. "That is another kind of asset I shall also be buying. There are men and women in the Capi-tol, and in the White House, who are today millionaires and even billionaires, but in a week they will be impoverished or bankrupt. The colonel has already drawn up that list. She has an impressive mind. Have you ever played chess with her?"

Maria looked away. "No, she has never played that kind of game with me."

"She thinks seven, eight—ten moves ahead all the time."

"So she has drawn up a list of congressmen, governors, members of the executive..."

He was nodding, gazing at the cruiser. "Yes, those who will be most useful, and those who will be worst affected by the collapse. Joe Olsen, for example, in Texas. He has been badly hit by the explosion in Midland, and his controlling shares in TexOl are in free fall right now."

"So next week you approach him and offer to buy controlling shares in TexOl, return him to financial solvency and take control of the company. You leave him as a director and thus you own the company and you also have your man in Congress."

"By early summer we will own not only the national infrastructure, we will also own the legislature, the executive and the judiciary."

She sipped her wine and watched the waiter bring out a platter of oysters. When he had gone she asked, "What about me?"

"I don't know." He swallowed an oyster and sipped his wine. "Ask the colonel."

"She just calls me *zaychik* and tells me she will always take care of me. Sometimes she even calls me *vozlyublennyy*.[1]" He chuckled. She glanced at him and said, with a touch of venom, "She hates you, you know."

"Of course I know. Fortunately for me I have no time for love or hate. These emotions cloud the mind. Need is more powerful than love—or hate."

She thought of José and how she had been able to control him and use him in spite of his needs. "Maybe," she said. Then she studied him a moment while he ate. "Has she instructed you to kill me afterwards?"

He didn't flinch. He shook his head. "No, but I wouldn't tell you if she had."

"You wouldn't, but your face might."

He chuckled some more. "How about you? Have you been instructed to eliminate me?"

"Not yet, but I expect it daily." She was pleased to see his brows contract briefly, and added, "It would be a shame."

"Would you do it?"

"Of course. What alternative would there be?"

He grunted, but she knew she had him thinking. She sipped her wine and after a moment said, "I think it is impossible to separate love from need. Love is just another kind of need, which is overlaid with romantic, sentimental mythology that hides its true nature. But at its root it is merely a need; a need for security, safety, certainty, physical touch perhaps, but ultimately it is just a need."

He nodded, gave a small shrug. "You are probably right."

"Can you imagine ever needing a person—one special person—in your life?"

"You mean apart from my investment manager and my tailor?"

"I am being serious, Peter. Do you ever think of the future, when you are too old for the job? It will come soon. In ten years, maybe twenty at most. Think, twenty years ago, the millennium. It seems like yesterday. When that time has passed again, where will you be? What will you be doing? Will you be alone? Loneliness is powerful and damaging. Even if we call it need instead of love, it is no less carcinogenic for that."

"*Carcinogenic?* No, I have never thought about it, but I suppose you are right. There will come a point where an expensive prostitute will not be enough. We will want someone to help us with the crossword instead of the bedroom Olympics. Are you proposing marriage to me, Maria?"

She laughed. "It could be fun. I was in love with you before I was forced to grow up. But I think I would need to trust my husband, Peter. And I could never trust you."

That night in their stateroom on board the *Princess Diana*, after dinner, she made him ask for sex before she yielded to him. Then she did not seek her own satisfaction, but focused all her attention on what he wanted, on what he needed. And when she heard him roar and cry out, when she felt him lose control, she smiled to herself and enfolded him in her arms, drawing his gasping head down to her breast.

In the morning they showered and dressed in silence, and at nine they breakfasted with the captain.

"What a shame you could only join us at Bermuda. We've had a superb crossing. It might have been the Med rather than the North Atlantic."

Peter made a wistful face. "Our intention was to board at Southampton, which is just a half hour's drive from Oakley."

A lady in a large straw hat and a floral dress asked in a piping voice, "Is that your house, Mr...?"

The captain interceded to avoid embarrassment. "Lord Oakley's ancestral home is just half an hour's drive from Southampton, Mrs. Grubber."

"Terrible draughty old pile," Peter said with a self-depre- cating laugh, "but we're fond of it, darling, aren't we? My god-knows-how-many-greats grandfather had the good sense to back Henry instead of Richard. War of the Roses, you know. So Henry gave him Oakley Park to build a house on, and made him Earl Oakley. So you see it pays to back a winner."

"We love it," said Maria, "and of course Hector and Achilles *adore* it." She laughed. "That's our dogs."

Peter went on, "So the plan was Southampton, but then Maria's father got sick in Spain, I had transactions to attend to in Turkey, we both had commitments in Croatia—" He started laughing out loud and everybody joined in. "So in the end we thought, 'We'll just get the boat in Bermuda!' It was quite the alliterative adventure, I can tell you!"

"Splendid!" The captain actually clapped. "Alliterative adventure. Very clever! Well, you must be exhausted, but I hope you will at least be able to relax on this last leg of your odyssey."

"We are very much looking forward to it, Captain. I can assure you of that. We are looking forward to taking the sun, having a splendid luncheon and doing very little else. Oh, and we mustn't forget, darling. This evening we have dinner with Dame Barbara at nine." He turned to the captain. "We will be on time for that, won't we?"

The captain looked vaguely worried. "If you go directly from the ship. Provided customs don't hold you up."

Peter blinked. "I hadn't thought of that. One gets so used to traveling light." He turned to Maria. "Well, look, darling. You'll have to go on alone and I'll see to the luggage. I'm sure it won't—"

She cut him short. "I can't turn up *alone*, Peter! Whatever will people think? The Earl of Oakley's wife, the Countess Oakley, turning up *alone* at the British Ambassador to the United Nations' dinner party! What *are* you thinking?"

There were eight people at the captain's table, and all of them but Peter and Maria turned to look at the captain. He mouthed like a goldfish for a moment, then said, "Well, I mean, how much baggage have you got?"

"Just four suitcases."

Maria pressed him. "You *really* should have thought of this before, Peter!"

"I know, I know. You're absolutely right. But I can't think how we can do this. We simply can't be late."

Again, six pairs of eyes fastened on the captain.

"Just four cases?" he said. "Well, I really shouldn't, but look, as it is a *diplomatic* matter, you just go ahead to her Excellency's dinner and I'll see to your luggage as though it were mine and have it sent to your hotel." He looked at his other guests and added hastily, "This is absolutely *not* something I would normally do. But we can't have the Earl and Countess of Oakley arriving late for the British Ambassador to the United Nations, can we?"

There was a general nodding and muttering of agreement, and everybody felt agreeably comfortable that they belonged to that section of society where the captain of your cruise ship, at whose table you are invited to dine, smuggles your luggage through customs so you can make it on time to the ambassador's dinner.

And that evening at eight PM Peter and Maria disembarked from the *Princess Diana* in the comfortable knowledge that their cases would enter New York through the back door, free from any customs checks. It had been a fair bet as it was that the Earl and Countess of Oakley would not be subjected to customs checks—and indeed that nobody would bother to check whether there existed such personages in the first place. The captain wouldn't care because he had sold his most expensive stateroom, and if the captain said they were the Earl and Countess of Little Piddle on the Puddle, nobody was going to argue.

But Peter's flash of inspiration had been typical of his genius. He had seen the potential in the situation and without a second's hesitation he had exploited it. As a result the cases would be sent directly to the Royal Suite at the Plaza, by the cruise company's own currier.

Their suite at the Plaza, which was costing the Kremlin forty thousand dollars a night, was just thirty yards from Central Park, four miles from Wall Street, just one mile from the United Nations building on United Nations Plaza, First Avenue. The location could not be better.

They made a point of going directly to the hotel and checking in, leaving instructions at reception for their luggage to be sent up as soon as it arrived. If it arrived while they were dining, the cases were to be stacked unopened in the wardrobe.

As it was, the cases arrived while Maria was showering. Peter tipped the boy and he and Maria unpacked three of the cases, so that they could dress for dinner. The fourth they placed together in the wardrobe. Then they fell on the bed together and had frenzied, animal sex just twelve feet from an atomic device which, in a few hours, would detonate and erase the city of New York from the map of the world.

Half an hour later they went down for a late dinner in the Palm Court. They had caviar, lobster and champagne, followed by rack of lamb and claret at eight hundred dollars a bottle. They made a noise, got noticed, tipped the waiters extravagantly and, when the restaurant closed, they transferred to their suite, where they ordered room service to the tune of several thousand dollars. By the time they collapsed into bed, the entire staff were aware that Lord and Lady Oakley were in the Royal Suite, they were big spenders and they were *not*, under any circumstances, to be upset.

Peter collapsed on the bed fully dressed. She removed his shoes and his jacket and left him snoring softly. Meanwhile she went to the dining room, poured herself the dregs of the coffee and telephoned Colonel Alexandrina Vitsin.

"You have taken too long to report."

"It was not possible till now. Things went much better than expected."

"Where are you?"

"In the Royal Suite, at the Plaza. We have dined and had room service. We have made an impression."

"The suitcase?"

"In the wardrobe."

"Where is Peter?"

"Sleeping."

"I do not trust him."

Maria knew better than to comment. "Is there some action you want me to take, Colonel?"

She was silent, then said, "He is charged with buying into the oil industry, and cultivating friends. Is that something you think you could do?"

"I have the appropriate training, Colonel. I will do whatever you order me to do without question."

"I know that, *vozlyublennyy*. You are my *detka zaychik*." She fell silent. Maria could hear her breathing, slightly ragged at the far end. When she spoke again it was almost a whisper.

"I get lonely sometimes, you know, Masha. Even a woman like me can become lonely. Does that surprise you?"

"I always think of you as so strong, *yubimaya mat*[2]."

"I must retire soon. Maybe we could buy a ranch in California, near the sea. You could live there with me and look after me as I grow old!" She laughed and to Maria it was like the screaming of a parrot in the jungle. Then more seriously she said, "If you took care of buying the assets for Mother Russia, we could take a good commission. Could be a lot of money, *zaychik*. We could have very fine life, you and me."

Maria fought furiously to inject feeling into her voice. "You are my *yubimaya mat*. I will always do what you tell me, *Mama*."

"Good girl, my good sweet girl. When the time comes, I will tell you."

SIXTEEN

Claire was trembling. She was biting her lower lip and I could see her knees were shaking.

"I heard Jamil and Chet talking..."

I snarled at her, "For someone who knew nothing and needed debriefing you sure as hell are remembering a lot of things you didn't know."

Over the phone I heard Nero say, "Alex, shut up and listen to her."

Her lips curled in, she held her breath and bit back the tears. "I didn't know," she said in a small squeak. "It was just Chet and some guy talking about deals. I didn't know it would be about all this!" She gestured helplessly at the whole room with both hands. "I don't *know* about any of this. I'm just trying to help!"

I said, "OK, I'm sorry. What do you think they said about disarming it?"

She closed her eyes, took a big slow breath and bit her lower lip with very even, white teeth. "He was sitting on the sofa, rolling a joint. So he had the phone on speaker. And Jamil was saying," she adopted a slightly Indian accent, "'Now I want you to listen very carefully, Chet. This is real important, OK? The case has a special locking mechanism, so nobody can steal the contents. When you receive it, it will be in the locked position, understood?'" She glanced at me. "It helps me to remember if I remember his voice. 'When you deliver it, you have to switch it to the open position. Otherwise they won't be able to open it.' So I'm figuring that that was all BS, because that's what the catches are for, right? I think he was telling him how to set the detonator."

Nero's voice said, "She could be right."

Claire said, "He made him do a couple of practice runs. I'm pretty sure I can remember."

I said, "Your call, Chief."

"What choices have we got, Alex?"

I actually thought about it and concluded what I already knew. "None. They're not going to evacuate the city, right? You're sure of that."

"I am sure of that."

"And if you warn them now, they'll run and leave the rest of us to fry."

"That is correct, Alex. They are politicians."

"Well, I don't think you've got time to warn them, Boss. This baby could blow any second." I looked at Claire. "You up for this? You want me to do it and you tell me how?"

She shook her head. "I'm more likely to make a mistake if I explain it. I can do it."

"Good girl. OK. Let's do it."

I stood back and she approached the case. It had its wheels facing her. She rubbed her fingers with her thumbs a few times, took a deep breath and took hold of the top, right-hand wheel. She pushed hard inward and turned it anticlockwise. I felt my heart jolt high up in my chest and we both froze. Nothing happened and she started to turn. The caster came free and revealed in the base, embedded in the case, a chip, a small LCD display, a few wires and a diminutive plastic switch. It was a bizarre mixture of the very basic and high tech.

"That's it?" I said. "That is what stands between us and..."

Nero's voice cut me short again. "Shut up, Alex."

"Yes, sir."

Claire was sweating. Her hands and her breathing were trembling. She looked at me and her eyes flicked over my face, like she was searching for something there. Something that would make this all right. I'm pretty sure she didn't find it.

"I have to flip that switch into the other position. Right now, if I'm right about what Jamil told Chet, the bomb is armed."

She reached for the switch. Her hand was shaking violently and I almost reached across and did it for her, but she stopped me, took a deep breath and flipped the switch with her small thumb.

We stood perfectly still. Nero's voice said, "For God's sake, what is happening?"

Claire said, "I think now the bomb is disarmed."

"Sir, she believes she has disarmed the bomb. She found the switch and changed its position, and we are still here. I think."

I had turned a moment toward the window while I was

speaking and, when I turned back, Claire had spun the case, released catches and opened the lid.

"*What the hell!*" I moved forward, reaching for the lid but she pushed my arm away.

"*No!*" she snapped. "You'll arm the damned thing again! It is safe to open once it's disarmed."

There was a flap inside. She lifted that too and there was exposed a shiny, steel or perhaps aluminum surface that fit the case perfectly. It had in it a small window with what looked like a digital clock that displayed four zeros.

"Sir, you had better send in your experts. I have never seen anything like this. And alert the cops to the situation. We need to seal the hotel. We really should evacuate it—and the city." I sent him several photographs and added, "You had better warn the president now, and leak it to the goddamned press!"

He hung up and I frowned at Claire, who was trembling violently. She took a hold of me, rested her head on my chest and squeezed hard.

"Hey," I said, "you did good. You were very brave."

She didn't answer. She just squeezed tight and I could feel her legs shaking. I figured she was going into shock, picked her up and carried her out to the corridor where I deposited her on a padded chair beside the elevator. As I did so I told the concierge, "Go back to reception. When the cops get here send them up. And I have some advice for you. I'm a really nice guy, but if you talk about this to anyone, the CIA will kill you. So I would forget the whole thing, if I were you. It never happened."

He looked at me as though I disgusted him, and people never said things like that in France. He stalked into the elevator and went down. Claire was sobbing into her hands and I was wondering how long the team would take to get there when my phone rang again. It was Nero.

"There have been more explosions."

I closed my eyes and sank down into a squat. "Where?"

"In Silicon Valley. The details are not clear yet. The explosions seem to have been massive. They have affected AI Solutions Incorporated, MicroMedia International, Nano Global, NASA, Microsoft, Moffett Airfield, the Google Campus, several of the NASA Ames buildings. Alex, how can they have done this?"

"Jesus Christ..." I rubbed my eyes. "With suitcases," I said. "It's like Russian Roulette. Each case is a chamber in the revolver, with an explosive charge, but each case is also a trigger for a different chamber. And you never know which one."

"Perhaps we should have used the EMP after all, as the general said."

"We disarmed this one, or so we thought, assuming the trigger to the bomb was *with* the bomb, but the triggers to the bombs are in *other* bombs. Somebody could walk into a hotel in LA right now—or anywhere in the USA—grab a case and detonate this bomb right here."

"Get out of the hotel. Evacuate the hotel. The police and our nuclear explosives experts are on their way."

I hung up and grabbed Claire. "Come on, we have to get out of here."

I didn't waste time with the elevator. We ran down the stairs, taking them three or four at a time. When we reached reception I found my French friend. His expression had not improved.

"I need you to do two things. First, get me the manager of the hotel, now."

"I have called him already. He is on his way. I don't know what he will 'ave to say about—"

"Shut up. Second. I need you to organize the staff—all the staff—and start evacuating the hotel. You collect everybody and you take them in an orderly fashion down to the memorial gardens. Take them to the Lincoln Memorial. You get them as far away from the hotel as you can. You understand? There is a bomb in this hotel, and it is a very powerful bomb."

"*Mon Dieu! La valise!*"

"Yeah, *la valise*. But God won't help you. You have to do this yourself. Make it happen. Now!"

As I said it sirens were wailing outside and a bunch of cops burst through the door. A guy in a suit with gray hair and a face like a summons strode toward me showing me his badge.

"Commander Phillips. You want to tell me what's going on?"

I showed him my small, plastic card and he arched an eyebrow. While he did that I said, "No. There's no time. You need to seal off the area for about four blocks in each direction—at least! You need to get the president and his family out of DC and you need to evacuate this hotel and all the buildings in the vicinity. There is a bomb in this building. It might be an SND and my office is sending an expert in nuclear devices. I hope I have made myself clear. Once we have those tasks done, I will explain further."

He didn't flinch. He looked real serious, but he didn't flinch. He was good. He was talking on the phone, delegating, giving orders and bit by bit the chaos of uniforms, waiters, chefs and concierges, and sleepy, scandalized guests, began to take shape into a coherent evacuation.

Meantime people kept arriving. The nuclear devices team showed up. I told Claire to stick to me like glue and we took them back to the room. On the way up I told them: "You're going to have to work with a dead guy on the bed. The crime scene officers can't come in till you're done."

They nodded like I'd told them the window was open because the air-conditioning was broken and their team leader muttered, "Let's hope he's the only casualty of the night."

We filed out of the elevator and I led them to the room, showed them the chip Claire had uncovered and told them what the general had told me about an EMP. They listened very carefully, then the team leader spoke:

"OK, we can't wait for you to finish your evacuation, because we know nothing about this bomb, how or when it will detonate. Please leave us to our work now and don't interrupt us. Get everybody as far away from here as you possibly can, as quickly as you can. Go now, please."

He was convincing and I left. All the way down the stairs my mind was spinning, working too fast for me to follow. And everywhere, all around us, there were streams of people, most complaining, others cajoling, others barking orders. It was impossible to hear my own thoughts.

I took Claire and we stepped out of the hotel into the night. It was no different out there. The sidewalk was packed and the cops were literally herding the people down 15th Street. While unseen, the city authorities fell out of bed and scrambled for the airport while they tried to think about where to put almost a million citizens, without further alarming the stock market.

And the president, as his chopper carried him away toward his bunker in Camp David, would be wondering what the hell he was going to tell the millions of investors who were propping up the American economy.

I stood a moment, with Claire by my side, watching the flow of people. There was a good chance, however far they went, that they would die tonight in a nuclear blast. And if the searing heat and the blast wave didn't get them, the radiation would. And whatever benefits one system might have over another: Left or Right, Democrat or Republican, Communist or Capitalist, in the end what they all had in common was that these were not people. They were consumers: units for the consumption of goods and the payment of revenue. The crime here, the monstrous crime, was not that Bill, or Tracy, or the twins, Grandpa or Aunty Peg were going to die a horrible death, it was not that children were going to be robbed of their parents, or parents robbed of their children. The crime, the heinous, monstrous crime, was that the American economy was going to be crippled.

I was not so naïve as to think that a crippled economy would not affect Bill, Tracy, the twins, Grandpa and Aunty Peg. But the point that was hammering at my mind and kept repeating itself over and over was that the *crime* here—the *actus rheus*[1], was that the American economy was going to be crippled. That was what the president was agonizing over and, by extension, it was what the Kremlin was delighting in. It was, in fact, the Kremlin's objective.

That was the point.

My cell rang again.

"Sir?"

"Alex, when did you last sleep or eat?"

"Um..." I tried to think. "I don't remember offhand, sir. Why?"

"Because there is nothing more you can do tonight. You should go home, try to get some sleep, eat something. If we have the good fortune to see tomorrow, I will need you in top form."

"Yes, sir." I hesitated a moment. "Sir, just in case. It has been a privilege working for you."

"Oh, yes, indeed, likewise. Of course."

"Sir?"

"Yes, Alex. I hope you are not going to become maudlin."

"No. If the target is not the people, but the economy, does that change anything?"

He was silent for a long moment. Finally he said, "It's a very good question, Alex. One I should have thought of myself. But, alas, I'm afraid it doesn't really get us anywhere, no."

I sighed. "I guess you're right. My brain is getting tired. Good night, sir."

"Good night, Alex. We'll catch up in the morning."

I hung up and muttered to myself, "Maybe in Valhalla."

"I'm sorry."

I looked at Claire and frowned. She repeated, "I thought I was defusing the bomb, and I've killed all these people, and achieved nothing."

I took hold of her shoulders. "Hey, no. You can't do that. You are not to take even an ounce of responsibility for what happened. You tried, as we all have, as Detective Macdonald did, to save lives. But the bastards who set this up did it precisely so that we would make these mistakes..."

I trailed off, hearing my own words, knowing they had a deeper, larger meaning but unable to grasp what it was. I shook my head.

"You are not responsible, Claire. You have been very brave and you have done nothing wrong. Come on, let's go and try to get some rest."

"Thanks."

She gave me another squeeze and we climbed in my car, which was still sitting on the sidewalk outside the hotel.

I drove slowly. The roads were empty but for the occasional cop car. They didn't stop us and there was no sign of a city-wide evacuation getting underway. We drove in silence through the stage-set streets lit by the tenuous amber lights that seemed to turn all the shadows it made into potential dreams. As we turned into Adams Street she said, "Are we going to die tonight?"

I pulled up and killed the engine before looking her in the eye. "No." Then I added, "But if we do, it will be instantaneous. We won't know anything about it."

"I want to know," she said. "When my time comes I want to know. Do you believe we continue living in another world? Or maybe we come back, reincarnated?"

"I don't know, Claire. All I know is that until our time comes, we need to keep fighting in this world."

"Yeah, I guess you're right."

"Come on. Let's get some rest."

SEVENTEEN

She made some hot chocolate and laced it with whiskey, and we sat for a while in the living room, in front of the cold grate. We didn't talk. We just sat and waited for the flash of blinding light, the seven-hundred-mile-per-hour radioactive wind, the utter extermination of the city.

After half an hour it hadn't happened. After an hour it hadn't happened either. So we went upstairs, she to the guest room and I to my bedroom. I brushed my teeth, stripped and fell into bed, mentally, physically and emotionally exhausted, but unable to sleep. I closed my eyes but my mind raced on at a thousand thoughts a second; and over and over again the notion came back to me: neither Washington nor Moscow sees them as people. The people are not the target.

The people are not the target.

I had not been lying down long when I heard a tap at the door. It wasn't a total surprise. I said, "Yeah, come in." It opened and she stood framed in the doorway, silhouetted against the filtered light of the landing outside. "What's up?"

"I keep thinking, if I am going to die tonight, I don't want to die alone."

I didn't know what to answer, but before I could even try she said, "Can I get in with you? Not for, I don't mean for..."

"Sure, come on, get in. Though you'll feel stupid in the morning. If it hasn't exploded by now, I don't think it's going to."

She slipped in beside me and I was alarmed to discover she had no clothes on.

"Shouldn't you put on a T-shirt or something?"

"No. I always sleep like this. Does it bother you?"

"No," I said, truthfully enough. "It's just, you know, there's like twenty years and no clothes between us."

"Hold me, please. Just put your arm around me. Just chill and hold me."

I chilled and held her.

"What are you thinking, Mason?"

"That you should keep still and let me sleep."

She giggled. "Is that how you want to look back on your last night on Earth? You were in bed with an attractive, nude twenty-year-old and all you wanted to do was sleep?"

"Cut it out, and keep still."

"Tell me what you're thinking."

"Honestly?"

"Yes, honestly."

"I keep thinking the same thing, over and over. That the target is not the people. That their aim is *not* to kill millions of people. If they die, that's collateral damage. The real target, the *real* target...hey, cut that out!"

"You know what I am thinking? I'm thinking I do *not*

want to spend my last night on Earth talking about targets and collateral damage. Tonight, either we live or we die, and there is sweet FA we can do about it. But *how* we spend that night, now *that* is up to us!"

———

IN NEW YORK, at the Plaza, Peter lay with his eyes open watching Maria sitting half naked by the window with the moonlight touching her nose and her cheek with turquoise light. She did not know he was awake. She was thinking that people were, as Sigmund Freud had said, the product of their childhood conditioning, and can never change the foundations of who they are. It was pointless to battle against a past that no longer existed. The traumas that shape you are *inside* you. They are the very fabric of your identity.

And yet. She said the words in her mind, *And yet...,* but only silence followed. Silence because her mind stopped speaking aloud, but it whispered and mouthed, and replayed movies of José being shot, replayed images and feelings of sleeping with Peter. Replayed feelings and emotions she had always assumed had withered and died in her.

So had she changed, contrary to Freud's law, or was there more to her conditioning than she had assumed? She looked back to her past, her childhood and her years of training as one of the colonel's agents, and in her mind she saw a dark swamp of shadows, mist and mire, and her feeling was of helplessness, powerless surrender, a complete absence of options besides those fed to her by Mother Russia, through the mediation of *yubimaya mat,* Colonel Alexandrina Vitsin.

But when she thought of the years she had spent with José, her sleeper years, she saw sunlight and she felt happiness. Had she loved José? She had always assumed she was incapable of love. But she missed him, she bitterly regretted his feeling of betrayal in those last seconds, and she missed him. Was that love? Did anybody know? Could anybody identify love—sit there and say this is, this is not, this is, that is not?

And did she love Peter? She was certainly attracted to him, and when she was not with him, she wanted to be with him. She knew he was bad, and ruthless and dangerous, but she didn't care about that.

She looked over at him and saw the light reflecting off his open eyes as they watched her. She didn't say anything, but looked back at the window. His voice came to her through the gloom.

"Did she order you to kill me?"

"No." And after a pause, "But she will."

"And will you do it?"

She gave a small, unhappy laugh. "That's what I was sitting here wondering."

"And?"

"What do you think?"

"I think you'll do it. Mother Alexandrina has a lot of power over you."

"Really? Maybe you have power over me too. Or maybe nobody has power over me. Maybe I just believe people have power over me, but actually the person who has power over me, is *me*."

"Be careful, Maria, that is dangerous thinking. Next

thing you'll be saying we should replace rights with liberties, and taxes should be optional."

"And people are more important than society."

"Heresy. The People are society and society is the People. All are one and Putin is the Father."

"You're mocking me, Peter."

"A little."

"Are you going to kill me before I kill you?"

He didn't answer straight away. When he did answer he said, "I don't want to. Do I need to?"

She looked at her naked knees, touched with moonlight, and placed her hands on them. "I tell you, 'No, you don't need to,' and you inform Colonel Alexandrina Vitsin of my betrayal, and she orders you to kill me. On the other hand I tell you, 'Yes, you need to because I am loyal to Mama Alexandrina,' and to save your own life you kill me. And in any case—" She shrugged and looked over at Peter with enormous sadness in her eyes. "Why would you believe anything I say? We are trained to lie, and we are trained never to believe what we are told."

"So without truth, what can we do?"

Suddenly she threw back her head and laughed out loud. "Is this going to be an epiphany for us? We will be liberated from existential servitude and discover that truth does indeed set you free."

He reached for a packet of cigarettes on the nightstand beside his bed, shook one free and lit up. He inhaled deeply and let out the smoke slow.

"Their great power is that they make us laugh at the possibility of our own freedom."

"Aren't you scared that I will report back to Mama Alexandrina?"

"I have never been afraid of her. She is a stupid old lesbian who belongs back in the Soviet era. Her time is coming to an end, Maria. Those who are strong enough and brave enough will replace her. Where will you be when that happens?"

"*That* is dangerous talk, Peter. I don't want to listen to it."

She stood and walked naked across the room to her wardrobe. There she pulled open the doors, reached inside her jacket and produced a long, slim-bladed knife which she removed from its sheath. She dropped the sheath on the floor and walked to where Peter had raised himself on his elbows to watch her. She took the knife by the blade and proffered the handle to Peter, who stared first at the hilt, and then up at Maria's face. She said:

"Drive the blade down behind my left collarbone. It will sever the carotid artery and the aorta, and it will pierce my heart. Death will come in a couple of seconds, but all the bleeding will be internal. If this is the only life I am going to know, I want it to end now. And if you are going to kill me, I want you to do it with my permission. I have never loved anybody, Peter, but perhaps in the last couple of days I have loved you. I do not want to kill you. I would rather you killed me."

He took the stiletto from her fingers, swung his legs off the bed and stood. Then he walked around to stand in front of her. He placed the point of the blade just behind her collarbone, at the apex of its curve, and looked into her eyes.

"Here?"

She nodded.

"Will it hurt?"

"Yes, a lot, but only for two or three seconds."

"You want me to do it?"

"No."

"What do you want me to do?"

"I want you to kiss me, and hold me, and tell me that you love me."

He placed the knife on her nightstand, picked her naked body up in his arms and settled her gently on the bed. Then he lay on top of her as her arms went around his neck and her legs entwined with his.

An hour later he lay beside her, watching the first pale graying of the sky. He was tired. It had been a long week, and a demanding week. He had known Maria for a long time, since they were in their teens. They had liked each other, back in the days when liking people was something you did without wondering whether one day you would have to execute them.

Then she had been sent to Europe, and he to England, to become new people, and they had lost touch with each other. It had been unsettling to see her again. It had been unsettling to discover that the attraction was still there, the liking was still there, and that it mattered to him what became of her. They all knew that the colonel was a vampire, but of all of them she had focused hardest on Maria, entering into her mind and possessing her, abusing her and making her believe it was a favor, a gift she was giving her.

It had been thrilling, and frightening, the discussion they had had. Finding trust was difficult. He looked at the pale sky. His eyes were growing heavy and he was enjoying the feeling of Maria close by his side. He drew her a little closer. She stirred and kissed his shoulder.

———

I LAY STARING at the paling sky through my bedroom window. Claire's head lay on my shoulder. There had been no explosion and, though I was obviously relieved, the fact troubled me. I eased her head onto the pillow and sat up. And as I sat and looked out at the predawn, suddenly it made sense. Not all of it, but the crucial part of it made sense.

I went down to the living room and called Nero.

"Do you know what time it is?"

"No. You haven't slept, have you, sir?"

"No. I was going to call you in an hour or so."

"No need. It was a dummy, right? With a detonator set for the Silicon Valley bombs."

"Yes."

"It was never DC, sir."

"I disagree, Alex. That's absurd. We discussed this at the beginning. This bomb tonight was simply a red herring. We were meant to find Art Bernstein's body, and we were meant to find the second Art Bernstein to make us believe we had found the right bomb. But it was all a red herring. We should investigate this girl of yours. There is another bomb in DC, Alex. Whoever has planned this has a terrifying intellect."

I waited till he'd finished and told him, "The real bomb is in Wall Street, or near Wall Street." He was quiet. "Sir, think about it. The target was never the US government, or the US people. The target was always the economy. The purpose, as they themselves told us very clearly but in different words, was to cripple it so they could buy our infrastructure. They are modeling the Chinese Belt and Road Initiative, but much more aggressively."

"Are you right...?"

"If I am, they don't want to kill off the president and all his officials, or Congress for that matter. They would rather cripple them economically and then buy their farms, their factories, their banks and their oil wells, and get them up and running again, having taken possession not just of the nation's economic, agricultural and industrial infrastructure, but also of the men and women who run it. The bomb is in Manhattan and they will detonate it today or tomorrow."

"Why? Why today or tomorrow?"

"Because we have had two explosions that have proved to be non-nuclear. That has caused panic on the stock market, but it has also raised questions about whether the nuclear bomb is real. A third non-nuclear explosion would have a 'cry wolf' effect. The next one has to be real, and the target, from the start, has been the stock exchange. They will detonate a nuclear device in or near Wall Street today or tomorrow at the latest."

"How could I have been so blind? How did I not see this?"

"As you said, sir. Whoever planned this is a terrifying genius. It was very cleverly concealed."

"You need to get to New York immediately. But...what in God's name are you looking for? A car with a trunk near Wall Street?"

"OK, we need to think, and decide, is this a suicide bomber? Or will they want time to get away?"

"Do they even know when the detonation will take place?"

"If they plan to give the bomber time to get away, then we are looking at the parking garages or hotels, where the cases can be concealed for a longer period without risk of being detected. Obviously they will be as near as possible to Wall Street and the Federal Reserve. That narrows the field."

"Yes, but so far they have not shown much concern for their agents. They have killed several of them in the last couple of days."

"True, sir, but they were recruits, not agents. Whoever is entrusted with this mission must be a high-ranking, trusted agent. Those they are less likely to eliminate."

"Fair enough, good, at least *you* are thinking. I will talk to the mayor and the governor. We want the NYPD crawling over the hotels and parking garages like ants. Anything else you can think of, call me. Meanwhile, get yourself to New York as soon as you can."

"I'm on my way, sir."

I climbed the stairs at a run and pushed into the bedroom. Claire was sitting on the edge of the bed looking rough.

"I woke up and you weren't there. I was scared." She watched me go into the bathroom and turn on the shower. "Dawn is breaking and we're still alive," she added.

"That's always a bonus." I caught movement in the corner of my eye, turned and saw her leaning on the door-jamb. In the stark light of the bathroom, first thing in the morning, I was surprised to see that she looked closer to twenty-five than twenty. Maybe more. We had a moment of silence, then I stepped into the shower cubicle and started soaping myself under the jets of hot water.

She called, "Can I help?"

"No. I'm in a real hurry. I'm going to give you some money. I want you to go as far southwest as you can for the next few days."

"I'm not a whore. I don't want your money."

"Fine, then go to San Diego at your own expense. But whatever you do, go to San Diego."

"What's in San Diego?" she called back.

"It's what's not in San Diego," I said and turned off the tap. I opened the cubicle door, grabbed a towel and started drying my hair. "Radiation," I said. "In San Diego there will be no radiation."

"So where will you be?"

"In New York," I said. "I'm going to be in New York."

EIGHTEEN

They had room service send up a breakfast of coffee and croissants. They ate in silence, watching each other. He noted how she added cream and brown sugar to her coffee, buttered her croissant and dunked it in the coffee before eating it. She noted how he broke the croissant and added nothing to it as he ate it piece by piece; just as he added nothing to the coffee, drinking it strong and black. They both interpreted and understood the same messages from the small things they observed. She would try to make life better, he took it as it came.

After breakfast he called down for reception to arrange a car for the day. Then they showered together in silence, dried each other in an almost ritualistic fashion, and dressed. Finally, while he methodically (and probably unnecessarily) wiped all the surfaces clean of fingerprints, she called the colonel.

"We are proceeding to the final stage, Colonel. There

will be no more communication now until after the event. Have you any final instructions?"

"Yes, execute Peter. I will come to USA next week and we will discuss your role in the acquiring of assets. For now, I do not trust him. Eliminate him."

"Yes, Colonel."

She hung up. Peter came in from the bathroom and she smiled at him. He took the red Samsonite case from the wardrobe, opened the door and they went down to the lobby where, at the reception desk, Peter signed for the car and collected the key.

"It is the red Jaguar parked right outside, sir. Can I help with your case?"

Peter smiled. "No, it's surprisingly light, thank you."

Outside, in the morning sunshine, he dropped the case in the trunk, they climbed into the car and took off at a sedate pace along West 59th, with the glorious superabundance of Central Park foliage on their right, and the towering, skyscraping elegance of Manhattan on their left. They smiled at each other, but they knew they must not speak.

At the Columbus Circle they took Broadway and followed it, via Verdi Square, all the way to the George Washington Bridge. As he turned onto the bridge she glanced at him and there was inquiry in her eyes. He acknowledged it, but said nothing, did not explain.

At the far end he took exit 74 for the Palisades Parkway. They followed the Palisades upriver for about five or six miles, taking it easy in the morning sun, with the massive, dark flow of the Hudson on their right. They came finally to the Alpine Lookout. Here he turned off the interstate and parked in the shade of some pin oaks. They climbed out and the doors slammed in the quiet, startling among the breeze and the birdsong. They stood for a while looking down at the enormous body of dark water, apparently motionless, but darkly and relentlessly moving.

He took her hand and led her down some steps to a winding path among the trees. They were alone. It was midweek and midmorning, the great gray mass were all engaged in generating income and revenue. They, the outsiders, were alone among the trees and the birds by the river.

He led her then off the winding path, still holding her hand, treading a carpet of brown pine needles among trees and small yellow flowers, to a clearing where there was a large rock on which they could sit and view the river and New York, far on the other side.

There, he held her shoulders in his hands and kissed her lightly. He placed her at the back of the rock, and sat with his back to her. Then he opened the top three buttons of his shirt, pulled back the collar and, from his jacket pocket, he withdrew the stiletto she had given him the night before. He placed the point just behind his left collarbone, with the hilt rising beside his left ear. He spoke to her for the first time that morning.

"You will not kill me, Maria, in a hotel bedroom in the middle of Manhattan, in the middle of a critical operation. Nor would I kill you in such a place at such a time. We are professionals. Here you can kill me with impunity and drive away without anyone noticing the body for hours, or even days. You can return to Manhattan, leave the case in a parking garage, and make for California. Now is your opportunity. Take the hilt in your hands."

"No."

"Do it, Maria. The only way I can ever trust you is if we come to the point where I cannot possibly save myself. Do you understand? Take the hilt. This is quite literally the moment of truth."

She took the hilt in both hands and he closed his eyes and placed his own hands palms down on his knees.

"If you are going to kill me, Maria, kill me now. If you do not kill me now, then you must turn your back on Mama Alexandrina forever."

He counted to fifteen slowly in his mind. Then he felt the blade rise and he heard her voice softly beside him. "Take it, I do not want it."

She came around and stood in front of him. He took the knife from her and got to his feet. Without saying a word she sat on the stone where he had sat a moment before and he took her position, standing behind her. She pulled back her collar and he placed the blade behind her left collarbone. In her mind she felt the sharp bite, the thrust of the metal plunging deep, biting into her heart. Fear burned in her stomach, but she was aware it was not fear of death, but fear of betrayal, of humiliation, of the unspeakable loss.

Then she felt the release of pressure as he removed the blade. He came round and took her hands, and they both walked to the edge of the precipice and looked down at the dark water. His gesture was almost careless as he tossed the weapon out, and they watched it spiral down and vanish into the eternal black.

Maria started to laugh and they embraced each other and stood a long time on the edge of the vertiginous drop, just holding each other and swaying from side to side. Eventually he told her, "I have never felt anything like this before."

In the car, driving back toward Manhattan, he told her, "I have set up companies in Panama. They are tiny, shell companies registered as though by British owners. When the time comes to buy assets, after the explosion, for every asset we buy for Russia, we will buy another for one of the shell companies. I have an accountant in Los Angeles who deals with Mafia, Sinaloa, our Mafia before that ass Putin marched into Ukraine; large corporations that need to whitewash a lot of money. He will take care of the books for us. Then we can disappear, create new identities, move to Belize, the Caribbean, wherever you like."

She nodded. "I will tell the colonel I killed you and dropped your body in the Hudson. We'll fly to LA, rent an apartment and you keep a low profile for a couple of weeks or a month while I make the buys. Meantime we arrange some ID papers—passports, driver's licenses, and when the time comes we drive across the border, Mexico, Belize." She laughed. "They will have no idea what happened to me, where I went."

They drove back down Broadway to the financial district and Peter made his way to a parking garage on Liberty Street, sixty yards from the Federal Reserve and about double that to the New York Stock Exchange. If countries had testicles, this would be the United States' balls: the source of all creative energy, drive, courage and aggression, and at the same time the most delicate, sensitive part of its anatomy. Peter took three minutes to open the hood and disconnect the battery, thus disabling the vehicle's GPS. Then he opened the trunk, removed the caster under the Samsonite case and switched on the detonator.

He stood staring for a moment at the enormity of what he had done. Maria came and stood close behind him. He felt her living warmth against his leg and his body, and the dead, icy cold of the action he had just taken, and for a moment he felt sick. They kissed hungrily. Then she held his face and they looked for a long moment into each other's eyes. They did not need to speak. They both understood. After a moment he closed the trunk and said, "We have time, but no time to waste."

NINETEEN

"I'M AFRAID I CAN'T LET YOU DO THAT."

I frowned at her, then frowned at the mirror and started combing my hair. "What are you talking about?"

"I can't let you go to New York on your own."

"Claire, you're cute, you're really sweet, last night was wonderful, though morally ambiguous would be more accurate, but this is not the movies and you need to come down to reality."

"That was a shit thing to say, Mason."

"I'm sorry."

"Are you saying I didn't help you? Are you saying you would have got this far without my help?"

"I am not saying that, Claire. I am saying you are a civilian whom I am supposed to be protecting, you are twenty...," I frowned at her again, wondering why she suddenly looked older, "whatever you are, and I cannot allow you to follow me around the country on what is a very dangerous, highly confidential job."

"You said yourself hundreds of thousands of people could die, maybe millions. And I am the only help you have. I am the only connection you have with the REDS."

I sat on the bed and started pulling on my pants. "You are a connection with the REDS? You want to explain that to me?"

"You know what I mean. I have heard conversations. I was able to identify Jamil Abbad, I found the hotel in DC..."

"I know, I know, I know, but it doesn't change a thing. You have helped and when this is all over you will probably get a Congressional Medal, but now you have to go and wait in San Diego, and stay safe."

She stamped her foot the way she had back in Texas, and clenched her fists. "*No!*"

I sighed, tried to ignore her and started buttoning my shirt

She started dressing, yanking on her clothes any old how. "You can't stop me from going to New York."

"Wrong. I can have you arrested."

"For God's sake, Mason! If this goes wrong, if something happens, I want to be with you!"

I stood and gripped her shoulders. "We cannot afford to get emotional. This is not the time. We have to remain cold and focused. Now *stop* this!"

"All *right!*" She stamped again and shook free from my hands. "*You need me to find that bomb!*"

I was getting frustrated and irritated, and I had more important things to be thinking about right then than this kid's fantasies. I brushed past her and snapped, "What the hell are you talking about?"

"I know where the bomb is."

I turned to stare at her, disheveled and half dressed. She was watching me fixedly and breathing hard. Before I could say anything she said, "Don't say anything patronizing, paternalistic or stupid. This is an opportunity you *cannot* afford to let slip by. How well do you know New York?"

"Pretty well."

"The bomb is going to be in the financial district in an area comprised between the Brooklyn Bridge and Rockefeller Park, South Cove, the Battery and the Elevated Acre. Make sense?"

She'd lost her New Zealand accent and her manner was suddenly completely different. It was as though she had been possessed by the spirit of an adult.

"Who are you?"

"That's not important."

"*Not important?*"

"Mason, listen to me. *Every-second-counts!* I know where the bomb is going to be and you *have* to take me there! *Now!*"

"Since when have you known?"

"We get in that car of yours. We burn rubber all the way to Manhattan. And on the way we will have a little over two hours for me to explain everything."

"And you had better have a damned good explanation."

"I don't know if it's a damned good one or not, but it's the one you're going to get. And you might just remember now and then that you would not have got this far without our help."

I was tying my shoes, but that made me stop. "*Our* help?"

She opened the wardrobe, grabbed my jacket and threw it at me. "My help!"

Sudden rage welled in my belly. "*We don't step out of this damned house until you tell me—*"

"*There is no time!*" She stormed around the bed and grabbed me by the collar of my shirt, shouting into my face. "*There is no time, Mason! We have to go and we have to go now!*"

I wrenched her hands from my shirt, grabbed my jacket and shrugged it on, staring back into her face.

"How do I know?" I snarled. "How do I know you don't work for them? How do I know this is not a red herring?"

She stepped up and thrust her face into mine so they were practically touching. "There is," she said, "no time." And as she spoke she reached into my pocket and pulled out the key to my car. Next thing she was trotting down the stairs and I was going after her. She pulled open the front door and stepped out into the predawn cool. I caught up with her at the car and took the key from her. As she climbed in the passenger seat she said, "I will not say another word until we are on the I-95, past Baltimore and doing at least a hundred."

As I headed north toward the I-95 I called Nero again and put him on speaker.

"Sir I am headed for New York. Can you have Lovelock provide Highway Patrol with make, model and license plate? I need to get there fast and I will be breaking the speed limit."

"I'll take care of it." He sounded haggard. "But I am afraid you are going to receive minimal cooperation. The president has been speaking with Putin and the Kremlin is adamant that this is a hoax on the part of a radical, communist terror organization, and that their intelligence services know for a fact that this organization has no access to nuclear devices. They point to the two conventional explosions as evidence."

"And the president believes them? What does the CIA say?"

"They say they simply don't know. Their analysts acknowledge that there is not a shred of evidence to support REDS' claim. The tactical demolition devices that went missing after the Soviet collapse disappeared decades ago. Nothing has gone missing since."

"That simply supports the theory that this comes from the Kremlin itself."

"But the Kremlin is adamant they have had nothing to do with it, and they claim that a general collapse of the Western economy would damage them economically as much as anybody else. They point out there is no longer an Eastern and a Western economy. There is only a global economy."

"Is that true?"

"Up to a point, but it would require a very detailed study to reach any kind of meaningful conclusion."

"So what does this mean, sir?"

"It means that the White House is more afraid of the economic crash that would result from what they call a 'panic response' than they are of a nuclear device which they are increasingly convinced does not exist."

"So...?"

"So there will be no mass searches of parking garages or

hotels tomorrow in Manhattan. In the words of your friend Jerry, 'So far all your panic searches have yielded are the destruction of an oil refinery, the devastation of Silicon Valley and the worst few days on Wall Street since 1929. From here on in we'll be managing this thing from the White House.'"

"Jesus Christ!"

"I am an atheist, Alex, but right now I will take any help I can get. What is your source? Not Jesus Christ, I hope."

"It's Claire, sir. She claims to know where the bomb will be this morning."

"How does she know?"

I glanced at her. "She won't tell me, but she speaks in the plural."

"Be very careful. She has apparently targeted you since Texas. It seems she needs you in order to get to the bomb. She may be an agent working for an ally, or it may be something quite different. We have to wonder why she won't come clean with you. I'll talk to my opposite numbers in the Five Eyes. Presumably she has left fingerprints and DNA at your house? We can check those with Five Eyes too."

He went silent for a while. Claire turned to look at the console, then glanced at me. Nero went on, "Be very careful. You need to ask yourself what she will do when she no longer needs you." He sighed. "Keep me posted, please."

She didn't, as I knew she wouldn't, say a word to me all the way to New York. Along the way I had plenty of opportunity to observe her, and realized she was one of those plastic people who can transform their appearance with a twist of their hair, a small amount of makeup and, most important of all, a subtle change in their attitude. I thought of Meryl Streep in *The Bridges of Madison County*, and *Death Becomes Her.*

"Are you MI6?"

She looked at me a moment with no particular expression. "The only thing I am going to tell you, Mr. Mason, is where that bomb is."

"Mr. Mason? What happened to stamping Claire?"

She didn't answer. She didn't speak again until we reached the George Washington Bridge. Then she told me to turn south and take Broadway all the way down to Liberty Street. It was early morning and the traffic should have been jammed. But Broadway was practically empty, and everywhere you looked you saw stores closed and a feeling of listless despair. The banner headlines on the newsstand on 86th and Broadway read "HOURS RATHER THAN DAYS SAYS EXPERT."

At Liberty Street she said, "Left," and glanced at her watch. "The parking garage." I entered and she said, "Third basement." So I went down to the third basement with the squeals from my tires echoing like lost banshees in the dirty, cavernous darkness. "Park there, at the end. Reverse into the space."

I killed the engine and suddenly clarity flooded my mind. I looked at her face, set like blonde granite, watching an empty space half a dozen lots down. I smiled and said, "So what happens now, you kiss me and stick a stiletto in my heart, like you did with poor Art?"

She turned and her eyes flitted over my face for a moment. She almost smiled. "It was the best thing that ever happened to him. If I hadn't come along he would have died of tragic old age. The only woman in his life was his mother."

"Who were you to him?"

"Anna."

"Have you any idea who you are, or have you forgotten?"

"Please, I can take anything but clichés."

"So what happens now?"

"There will be two of them, a man and a woman driving a red Jaguar. He is tall, blond, English. She is shorter, dark. I shoot her, you take care of him. He is by far the more dangerous of the two. Then I disarm the bomb."

I sighed loudly and rubbed my face with my palms. "OK, I am going to get a serious migraine. You just told me you killed Art Bernstein. Now you want me to kill the guys who are setting the bomb. But that's you!"

"Jesus, Mason! I thought you were supposed to be smart!"

"You're like AI with faulty circuits. Will you please stop changing personalities? Who the hell are you?"

She groaned and rolled her eyes. "Hel-lo! Claire? I slept with you last night? I have *really* not got time for this! OK, pay attention. We have just a few minutes, if that. Caroline Popova, Russian counterintelligence, SVR. I am truly astonished that you are not aware that the Russian Federation is on the brink of a civil war. Do you seriously believe that after the fiasco of Ukraine, the Russian Executive would allow Putin to carry out this madness unopposed?"

"Yes."

"Well, you're wrong. There will be a coup in Moscow in

just a few weeks, if not sooner. And it is my job to stop Peter and Maria from detonating this bomb."

"Is that why you killed poor Art?"

"I had to kill him."

"Why?"

"Because Maria had seduced him and he was going to inform her I was here. Shut up, here they are."

The banshees had started screaming again, and after a moment a bright red Jaguar pulled into the aisle and parked in the space she had been watching.

"How did you know they were going to park there? How did you know they would be in this parking garage? How—"

"Shsh! Not now!"

An attractive couple got out of the car. She looked Mediterranean, he was tall, athletic and Scandinavian blond. He popped the hood and seemed to look at the engine, but I couldn't make out what he did. Then he closed the hood and opened the trunk.

Inside the trunk I could make out a red suitcase. I reached for the handle but she said, "No! Wait!"

"What the hell for?"

"Just wait!"

He did something to the case, then stood staring for a moment. The woman came and stood close behind him. He turned to her and they kissed. Then he closed the trunk and said something to the woman.

I said, "Screw this!" pushed open the door and got out. I heard Claire swear behind me and ignored her. I spoke loudly as the couple turned to look at me. "Peter and Maria?"

His accent was the upper-class English drawl. "Who are you?"

In an easy, fluid movement I pulled the Sig from under my arm and pointed it at the woman. I had seen the way he kissed her and there was no mistaking he had feelings. Then I answered his question, "I'm the man who's going to kill this woman if you don't deactivate the bomb in that red suitcase."

The woman took hold of his arm. Her expression was one of horror. His was a strange mixture of astonishment and delight.

"How..." he said, but trailed off as he looked over my shoulder. "Oh, Anna," he said. He placed his hand on the dark woman's arm, where she held him. It was a sad, kind gesture. "It was short but it was beautiful, Maria. I told you Alexandrina was always seven moves ahead." He looked at me and saw my frown. "Who are you?" he asked. "CIA? Do you know who Anna is?" He laughed, reading my face. "Maria thought I was detailed to kill her once the bomb was set, and I thought she was detailed to kill me. But Alexandrina foresaw the risks and sent Anna to dispose of us both. This is how it is today in Russia."

"Enough!" It was Anna behind me. "Shoot them both, Mason!"

"Are you out of your mind?" To Peter I said, "Open the trunk and deactivate that bomb, Peter. I will count to three, and on three I blow off her kneecap. You'd better believe I am serious."

"I believe you are serious," he said, and in the next second he had lunged at me. The Sig went off, the round hit the floor and whined into the blackness. I felt a searing pain in my left arm and hit the floor. I looked up and saw chaos and pandemonium. Peter was wrestling with Claire and one of them was trying to wrench a semi-automatic from the other's hands. But the pain in my arm made it hard to tell. Then Maria was there, tearing at Claire's blonde hair. I struggled to my knees and went to stand when Claire clawed the pistol from Peter's hands. She staggered back with Maria scratching at her face, but I could see Claire was swallowing the pain and had a bead on Peter. And I needed Peter alive. I took aim one-handed at a moving target and fired at Claire's gun hand. At the same instant Claire wrenched free from Maria's hands and staggered forward. The 9mm slug thumped into her temple and erupted out the other side, and Claire fell to her knees, then keeled over sideways.

I kept the gun trained on Peter. I spoke quietly. "Enough. Enough killing. There are nine million people in this city, human beings, children, babies, pregnant women, grandparents...for crying out loud, look inside yourself and find some humanity." The pain in my arm was threatening to knock me out. I fought to hold onto consciousness. "I saw how you held her. I saw how she held you back. I know you have it in you. You cannot live with nine million deaths on your conscience."

Then I forced myself to my feet. "And if you can, then I am going to blow your damned knees off and I'll sit you in that damned car till the bomb explodes with you in it."

"That won't be necessary." It was Peter. "I won't bore you with the story, as we are in a bit of a hurry. But when you saw us kissing, we had decided to deactivate the device." He moved to the trunk and opened it, and showed me the case. The screen was inactive and the switch showed in the off position. "Maria and I have decided to make a new start, Mr...."

"Mason."

"Mr. Mason. We will be sending a report to your relevant authorities, which should give you some leverage over Mr. Putin and his gang." He hesitated. "We are not saints, Mr. Mason, we are professional agents, but we want no more part of that ugly world that they have created. It is too long a story to try and convince you, but—" He pointed to my shoulder. "I don't think you are in a position to try and stop us, and I know you won't shoot us in cold blood."

"Don't be so damned sure," I said with not much conviction.

"If you give me your card, we can send our report to you. You have the bomb and all the facts. You don't need us."

It took me a full fifteen seconds to make up my mind. Then I handed him my card and watched them both walk away and disappear into the gloom.

EPILOGUE

THE GLOOM HAD TURNED TO BLACKNESS AND when I opened my eyes next I was in a hospital bed and felt kindly toward the whole world. Nero was there looking vast and scowling at me. And I was surprised enough to frown at Gallin, who should not have been there. I decided to ignore her and see if she went back into my head and looked at the bowl of fruit, the vase of flowers and the small fluffy teddy bear on my nightstand.

I smiled fondly at Nero, who was still scowling. "Did you buy me a teddy bear, sir?"

"Certainly not."

I turned the maudlin smile on Gallin. "So you really are here?"

"Yup. They have you on morphine. It was a miracle the slug didn't bust an artery and pierce your lung."

"That's nice."

Nero said, "I suppose you are incapable of coherence at the moment. How long will you be in this state?"

"How long *have I been* in this state?"

"Twelve hours."

"Peter," I said, offering Gallin a really soppy grin, "and Maria fell in love."

They both said simultaneously, "Oh, God!"

"And they are sending me a detailed report. I might have it already. And if I have, I will let you both read it."

Gallin narrowed her eyes and looked out the window. Nero grunted. "Will it incriminate Putin? Dammit!"

"Yup."

"You're sure of that?"

"Yup."

"But seriously, you guys," I said, "it is important to tell the people you love that you love them. And I love you both."

I heard Nero grunt something about "*Intolerable!*" and the door slam closed. Then I opened my eyes again and saw Gallin's beautiful face looming over me. She whispered, "I agree," and sent me off to sleep again with a kiss.

When I drifted back she was reading a magazine over by the window. I frowned at her and she shook her head. "It was a dream," she said.

I smiled and shut my eyes. "I'm going to see if I can have it again."

Don't miss EXECUTIVE ORDER. The riveting sequel in the Alex Mason Thriller series.

Scan the QR code below to purchase EXECUTIVE ORDER.

Or go to: righthouse.com/executive-order

NOTE: flip to the very end to read an exclusive sneak peak...

DON'T MISS ANYTHING!

If you want to stay up to date on all new releases in this series, with these authors, or with any of our new deals, you can do so by joining our newsletters below.

In addition, you will immediately gain access to our entire *Right House VIP Library,* which currently includes *ORIGINS*—a full length prequel novel to *ODIN.*

righthouse.com/email

(Easy to unsubscribe. No spam. Ever.)

ALSO BY DAVID ARCHER

Up to date books can be found at:
www.righthouse.com/david-archer

ROGUE THRILLERS
Gates of Hell (Book 1)
Hell's Fury (Book 2)

JACOB HUNTER THRILLERS
The Kyiv File (Book 1)
The Bogota File (Book 2)

PETER BLACK THRILLERS
Burden of the Assassin (Book 1)
The Man Without A Face (Book 2)
Unpunished Deeds (Book 3)
Hunter Killer (Book 4)
Silent Shadows (Book 5)
The Last Run (Book 6)
Dark Corners (Book 7)
Ghost Operative (Book 8)

ALEX MASON THRILLERS
Odin (Book 1)
Ice Cold Spy (Book 2)
Mason's Law (Book 3)
Assets and Liabilities (Book 4)
Russian Roulette (Book 5)

Executive Order (Book 6)
Dead Man Talking (Book 7)
All The King's Men (Book 8)
Flashpoint (Book 9)
Brotherhood of the Goat (Book 10)
Dead Hot (Book 11)
Blood on Megiddo (Book 12)
Son of Hell (Book 13)

NOAH WOLF THRILLERS

Code Name Camelot (Book 1)
Lone Wolf (Book 2)
In Sheep's Clothing (Book 3)
Hit for Hire (Book 4)
The Wolf's Bite (Book 5)
Black Sheep (Book 6)
Balance of Power (Book 7)
Time to Hunt (Book 8)
Red Square (Book 9)
Highest Order (Book 10)
Edge of Anarchy (Book 11)
Unknown Evil (Book 12)
Black Harvest (Book 13)
World Order (Book 14)
Caged Animal (Book 15)
Deep Allegiance (Book 16)
Pack Leader (Book 17)
High Treason (Book 18)
A Wolf Among Men (Book 19)
Rogue Intelligence (Book 20)
Alpha (Book 21)

Rogue Wolf (Book 22)
Shadows of Allegiance (Book 23)
In the Grip of Darkness (Book 24)

SAM PRICHARD MYSTERIES
The Grave Man (Book 1)
Death Sung Softly (Book 2)
Love and War (Book 3)
Framed (Book 4)
The Kill List (Book 5)
Drifter: Part One (Book 6)
Drifter: Part Two (Book 7)
Drifter: Part Three (Book 8)
The Last Song (Book 9)
Ghost (Book 10)
Hidden Agenda (Book 11)

SAM AND INDIE MYSTERIES
Aces and Eights (Book 1)
Fact or Fiction (Book 2)
Close to Home (Book 3)
Brave New World (Book 4)
Innocent Conspiracy (Book 5)
Unfinished Business (Book 6)
Live Bait (Book 7)
Alter Ego (Book 8)
More Than It Seems (Book 9)
Moving On (Book 10)
Worst Nightmare (Book 11)
Chasing Ghosts (Book 12)
Serial Superstition (Book 13)

CHANCE REDDICK THRILLERS
Innocent Injustice (Book 1)
Angel of Justice (Book 2)
High Stakes Hunting (Book 3)
Personal Asset (Book 4)

CASSIE MCGRAW MYSTERIES
What Lies Beneath (Book 1)
Can't Fight Fate (Book 2)
One Last Game (Book 3)
Never Really Gone (Book 4)

ALSO BY BLAKE BANNER

Up to date books can be found at:
www.righthouse.com/blake-banner

ROGUE THRILLERS
Gates of Hell (Book 1)
Hell's Fury (Book 2)

ALEX MASON THRILLERS
Odin (Book 1)
Ice Cold Spy (Book 2)
Mason's Law (Book 3)
Assets and Liabilities (Book 4)
Russian Roulette (Book 5)
Executive Order (Book 6)
Dead Man Talking (Book 7)
All The King's Men (Book 8)
Flashpoint (Book 9)
Brotherhood of the Goat (Book 10)
Dead Hot (Book 11)
Blood on Megiddo (Book 12)
Son of Hell (Book 13)

HARRY BAUER THRILLER SERIES
Dead of Night (Book 1)
Dying Breath (Book 2)
The Einstaat Brief (Book 3)

Quantum Kill (Book 4)
Immortal Hate (Book 5)
The Silent Blade (Book 6)
LA: Wild Justice (Book 7)
Breath of Hell (Book 8)
Invisible Evil (Book 9)
The Shadow of Ukupacha (Book 10)
Sweet Razor Cut (Book 11)
Blood of the Innocent (Book 12)
Blood on Balthazar (Book 13)
Simple Kill (Book 14)
Riding The Devil (Book 15)
The Unavenged (Book 16)
The Devil's Vengeance (Book 17)
Bloody Retribution (Book 18)
Rogue Kill (Book 19)
Blood for Blood (Book 20)

DEAD COLD MYSTERY SERIES
An Ace and a Pair (Book 1)
Two Bare Arms (Book 2)
Garden of the Damned (Book 3)
Let Us Prey (Book 4)
The Sins of the Father (Book 5)
Strange and Sinister Path (Book 6)
The Heart to Kill (Book 7)
Unnatural Murder (Book 8)
Fire from Heaven (Book 9)
To Kill Upon A Kiss (Book 10)
Murder Most Scottish (Book 11)

THE OMEGA SERIES

ABOUT US

Right House is an independent publisher created by authors for readers. We specialize in Action, Thriller, Mystery, and Crime novels.

If you enjoyed this novel, then there is a good chance you will like what else we have to offer! Please stay up to date by using any of the links below.

Join our mailing lists to stay up to date -->
righthouse.com/email
Visit our website --> righthouse.com
Contact us --> contact@righthouse.com

facebook.com/righthousebooks
x.com/righthousebooks
instagram.com/righthousebooks

EXCLUSIVE SNEAK PEAK OF...

EXECUTIVE ORDER

CHAPTER 1

I DROPPED THE NEWSPAPER ON THE SEAT NEXT TO me as the train came to a halt at Union Station, in Washington DC. There was a brief scream of tortured steel that echoed under the vaulted ceilings above, a jolt and then a big sigh as the train seemed to deflate and the doors hissed open.

I stood, grabbed my leather bag and made for the exit where a group of passengers had become logjammed. I paused to wait and somebody collided with me from behind. I turned and an attractive young woman smiled at me. "I'm so sorry," she said, "I wasn't looking where I was going."

Her eyes were an intense green, which with her strawberry-blonde hair made her face startling. She had a Cupid's bow mouth and a smile you wanted to keep talking to. I smiled back and stood aside. "Please, after you. I am not in a hurry."

She gave a shy nod, slipped past me, dodged through the logjam and, through the train window, I watched her trot away through the crowds. By the time I eventually stepped out onto the platform she was gone from view and had largely slipped from my mind. I found a cab and told the driver, "The Commonwealth Tower on Wilson Boulevard, across the river."

The drive was uneventful, along Constitution Avenue and over the Theodore Roosevelt Bridge, where the Potomac moved heavy and slow, rich with broken early morning light. We negotiated Spaghetti Junction and pretty soon we pulled up outside the Commonwealth Tower. I paid him the fare and reached in my jacket pocket for some coins to make up the tip, and that was when I found the neatly folded piece of paper.

I walked into Nero's office in the 1I section of the ODIN maze on the top floor of the tower, frowning at the piece of paper. The door closed behind me with a soft hiss and I continued to frown at it. After a moment Nero's voice intruded on my thoughts and I looked up.

"Have you arrived yet, or is it just your body that has walked through the door?"

I held up the piece of paper. "A list."

"Are you being deliberately cryptic in the hope of annoying me?"

"No." I sat. "It's a list of names. A couple are familiar, others I don't know. It's a photocopy of an original."

I slid it across the desk. For a moment he ignored it and simply watched me with what you could only describe as baleful eyes. Then he reached for the list and looked at it.

"Helen Troy," he said, reading the name at the top of the list. "The candidate for nomination?"

He glanced at me and I shrugged. "I have no idea. I found it in my pocket when I paid the cab downstairs. I don't think Helen Troy is a common name, so it is likely to be her."

He grunted softly. "You'd think most people with the surname Troy would have the good taste not to call their daughter Helen." He studied the list a moment longer. "Frank Costello and James Reed are also candidates for nomination in the same party. Recent leaks about Costello's ties with the Mafia have damaged him less than expected." He glared at me under an arched brow, like it was my fault. "Robert de Niro and Al Pacino seduced the American public into a love affair with the Mafia that endures to this day." He looked back at the list. "The clear favorite is James Reed, however. We still prefer our leaders to be from Anglo-Saxon or Irish stock. Troy lags behind the other two. Why is her name underscored?"

He sank back in his chair, inhaled deeply through his nose and held the piece of paper as though it were Yorick's skull.

"The first three are candidates for nomination. The next, Paul Hirschfield, is not an uncommon name. There is a Paul Hirschfield attached to the Israeli Embassy. He is a colonel in the Mossad. Israel has let it be known, quietly, that they favor Reed because his stance on Islam and Israel is unambiguous, whereas Troy and Costello are more wishy-washy. Priti Anand could refer to the American-born Indian financier. The Anands are billionaires and she has established herself as one of the richest, and most powerful women in America. And Johannes de Jong, born in South Africa, became a dotcom billionaire at twenty-one. Now, since the stock market crash you failed to stop this spring, he owns controlling shares in AI Incorporated, Cyber-Solutions and Tex-Oil."

He looked over the piece of paper at me and I smiled sweetly.

"My shoulder still hurts when the wind blows from the east."

"What, aside from this piece of paper, connects these people?"

"The first three are members of the same party, the last two are prominent financial backers of that same party, and Colonel Hirschfield supports that party quite vocally because that party supports Israel. So the party connects all the people on the list."

"Correct, but there must be more. I shall make discreet inquiries as to which of the candidates Anand and de Jong plan to back." He pressed a buzzer on his desk. When Lovelock's lovely voice oozed, "Yes, sir?" he snapped, "Come!"

The door opened and she entered, looking as lovely as she sounded. He handed her the list. "Copy this to the Archive and get them to send me everything they have on these people. Have them send it to Analysis too, and tell the spotty fellow," he waved his fingers at his head, "the one with greasy, unwashed hair—"

"Graham—"

"Graham, have him and Navneet analyze it. I want to know what has caused these names to be present together on this list."

"Yes sir."

She gave me an immoral wink and left on immoral legs.

Nero watched the door close and mused, "Navneet. It makes you wonder, what conjunction of social forces drives a parent to name his son 'Fresh Butter.' They could have called him Ravi, God of the Sun, they could have called him Pranav, Sacred Syllable, or even Son of Lord Buddha, Rahul. But no," he shook his head, "they called him Fresh Butter."

"Sir?"

He shifted his eyes to meet mine. "Think, how did you come by this list?"

"I think it was slipped to me when I was getting off the train at Union Station."

"Reason?"

"A young woman collided with me from behind. She was sweet and pretty and hurried on ahead of me."

"That is your reasoning?"

"That, and the fact that nobody else got that close to me from when I left Gallin at the hotel in New York until I arrived in DC."

"Gallin..." He drummed his fat fingers on the desk. "It is too much of a coincidence that she is a katsa and there is a Mossad intelligence officer on that list, and you are slipped the list returning from seeing Captain Gallin. But what does it mean? None of these others are connected to the Mossad, as far as I know."

"She's still in New York, you want me to talk to her?"

"No. I don't want you to talk to anyone until we know more. I am troubled also by the fact that Helen Troy's name is underscored twice, making her some kind of priority. Whoever wrote this list wrote her name and then wanted to express, 'Especially her,' or 'First her,' 'In particular *her!*'"

"You're thinking it's a hit list."

He pursed his lips and nodded, then gave a "maybe" shrug. "It could be." He flapped a hand at me. "Very well.

Go and see Senator Troy. Telephone Captain Gallin and ask her if she has any idea why the colonel's name should appear thus on a list with members and supporters of this party. Please mention no other names. See what she has to say."

"Yes sir." I went to stand but hesitated a moment. "You wanted to see me about something, sir. That's why I came back from New York..." I tried not to sound resentful.

He made an affirmative grunt. "Your friends who planted the suitcase bomb[1], and whom you allowed to get away, they have surfaced in Brazil."

"I was injured, sir, and it seemed to me that confirming that the nuclear device was deactivated was more..."

"Never mind," he interrupted me. "The information the CIA have is that they both died in a car crash near Belem. Dental records and fingerprints confirm it is them, though the bodies were burned beyond recognition."

"Oh." I nodded. "Rough justice."

He gazed at me a moment. "You're sentimental at heart, Alex. It's your only real weakness. That and a lazy mind." He drummed his fingers on the desk a moment, then went on. "It seemed a little convenient to me, so I had our operative inquire a little deeper and he confirmed they were alive and well living in Belize as Mr. and Mrs. Sedgemore. Discreet inquiries at the CIA and in Russia reveal that both are satisfied Peter and Maria are dead[2]."

"But..."

"Naturally it was my duty to consider requesting that Cobra review their case for possible crimes against humanity."

"Cobra?"

"Never mind. An agency you don't need to know about.

But in the end I concluded that our operative must have been mistaken, and I have closed the file on them. I trust you approve."

"I do, sir. I don't believe in epiphanies, but these two were the exception that confirmed the rule. They could have made billions by allowing the bomb to explode, but they defused it. I think that calls for a second chance."

He gave me a long level look, then said in a flat, dead voice, "And besides, they are dead."

"And that, too."

"Go and see Ms Troy. Sound her out, don't mention the list. See if any of the names mean anything to her. Talk to your friend, Captain Gallin. No names. Leave."

I left but paused on my way out to get Helen Troy's address from Lovelock and ask her, "Why do people make lists, Lovelock?"

She arched a devastating eyebrow at me. "Is this a 'women love shopping' question? You should know I self-identify as a woman who does not like shopping." I sighed and made for the door. She stopped me with, "I once made a list of men I might be unfaithful to my husband for."

I paused and looked back at her. She was smiling and winked.

"You weren't on it, honey. There was only one name on it, Sean Connery, but he was already in his seventies."

"Mish Moneypenny," I said, arching an eyebrow of my own, "shay it ain't show."

I rode the elevator down to the parking garage to collect my Factory Five Mk4 Roadster. I lowered the hood and rumbled out into the early summer sunshine still thinking about lists. It struck me that people made lists for just three reasons. In all three cases it was to have a precise collection of data handy, either A) to refer to it in some task like writing a book or putting together a piece of furniture, B) to be able to pass that data on, as in teaching a class, or C) to be able to eliminate those data from your list, as in a to-do list, a shopping list, or a hit list.

I told Siri to call Gallin. She was as cheerful as ever and made the call.

"So soon, already? You know there is nothing less attractive than a needy guy, Mason. Except maybe a drunk guy with sleep apnea."

"Are you done?"

"I just don't want you to ruin what could be a beautiful friendship."

"Now are you done?"

"Jeez! Get on with it! What do you want?"

"Why would Colonel Paul Hirschfield be on a list?"

"What kind of list?"

"A list I am instructed not to share with you, but which holds candidates for nomination, all in the same party, a couple of billionaires who are known to back that party, and the colonel."

"I need in."

"One step at a time, Sweet Aila. Does it make any sense to you that he is on that list?"

She didn't answer for a moment, then said, "What? No. I'll call you back. Wait. Where did you get hold of this list?"

"That's the trouble with this relationship, see? I give, give, give, and you always hold back."

She sighed as I turned onto the George Washington Memorial Parkway and started to cruise comfortably beside the river. "OK," she said, "no, Alex, on the face of it I cannot think of any particular reason why Paul should be on a list, except that several hundred million people would probably like to assassinate him. So, unless you give me more data, I can't help you."

"Being married to you would be a nightmare."

"I agree. Now, unless you are going to give me more data I am going to call my dad so he can call your boss and make you give me more."

"Fine."

She hung up as I left the Three Sisters behind me and was enveloped by trees. Fifteen minutes later my phone rang. It was Nero.

"Alex—"

"Yes, sir."

"I have just had the head of the London field office of the Mossad on the telephone to me."

"Yes, sir, Gabriel Gallin."

"Quite so. Good man. We've been friends for many years. Master chess player. Superb palate."

"Yes, sir. And Captain Gallin's father."

"Indeed. He feels the business of the list may have security implications for Israel. Colonel Hirschfield may be a target."

"Yes, sir. We had pretty much come to that conclusion ourselves, hadn't we? But do I gather you have changed your mind about briefing Captain Gallin?"

"No. I never change my mind, Alex. I have simply reassessed the facts. She'll be joining you here in DC. Read her in."

"Yes, sir."

He hung up.

It was a delightful drive up to Great Falls. There were more trees than people, which is always a good sign. Also, it was one of those places where the creatures who had inflicted the Great Hive of the grid system on the American people lived, happily and comfortably, among random, asymmetrical lanes and drives which adapted organically to the homes they served, creating a natural, spontaneous beauty, rather than defining the cubicles in which "the people" had to live in order to derive the greatest efficiency from their existence. Here the streets were not A, B, C or 1, 2 and 3. Here people lived on River Bend Road and Cornwell Farm Drive, and Little Piddle Lane. And as I weaved and wended my dappled way toward Jackson Lane, I felt certain nobody here would ever commit an impolite crime, and whatever crimes they did commit, they would never be so vulgar as to get caught.

Helen Troy's mansion was a vast jumble of neo-Victorian gables, turrets and faux-leaded windows that only needed a little lightning to be cast in an Addams Family movie. It was set among sweeping, well-behaved lawns against a backdrop of abundant trees that would not have been out of place in Vermont. There was, sadly, no twelve-foot wall and no iron gate guarded by ravens, and no lightning or thunder as I parked outside the door. There was however, a small distance away, outside the double garage, a small Toyota and the big Jaguar which was being washed by a huge black guy with his sleeves rolled up over arms like tree trunks.

I climbed from my Roadster and crossed the well-behaved lawn to ring on the doorbell. It was not opened by a hunchback with one eye, but by a pretty, South American maid in a pretty blue uniform with a white apron. Privilege will bring you these mundane pleasures.

"Good morning," she said, smiling like she really believed it was one. "Can I help you?"

"Yes," I told her. "I need to talk to Ms. Troy."

"You have an appointment, Mr...?"

"I don't need one," I said pleasantly. "Mr. Mason, Alex Mason. You could tell her I am here from the Office of the Director of Intelligence Networks."

I showed her my card and she nodded at it, then ushered me in and showed me to the office.

"Please, wait here. I will tell her."

The office looked like she'd taken a photograph of the Oval Office and tried to recreate it in her home. Maybe she had. The carpet was blue, the desk was walnut and set in front of three tall windows, there were two cream sofas perpendicular to the desk and there was even a portrait of Benjamin Franklin on the right as you looked at it.

After a couple of minutes the door opened and the woman who had been causing so much talk and speculation in the media was standing looking at me. She was in a pair of Levis that looked very happy to be where they were. She had on a plaid shirt with the sleeves rolled up and she was holding a wooden spoon with cake mix on it.

"Who are you," she said, "and what do you want?"

CHAPTER 2

AT ABOUT THE TIME GALLIN HUNG UP ON ME TO tell her dad to talk to my boss, Colonel Paul Hirschfield was organizing his pens in the walnut penholder his wife—his *ex*-wife—had given him for his fifty-eighth birthday. Red pens on the left, blue pens on the right. He smiled and shook his head sadly in a way only Jewish people know how to do, and considered the recent American practice of making Republicans red and Democrats blue. All his life the reds had been the Commies, the bad guys. Now the reds were the Republicans. You just didn't know who to trust anymore.

Recent! He snorted softly to himself. Twenty years ago! They had started referring to "red states" and "blue states" more than twenty years ago! Time. Time must be a woman because she was the greatest and most subtle traitor of all! He nodded and smiled. He liked that. He made a note, using a blue pen on a small notepad he had started carrying around with him since he'd decided to write his memoirs. He'd like people to remember him not just as a right-wing hawk, but also a man with a sensitive, poetic streak. And wit! Wit was important.

He put the pen back and called his wife. His ex-wife. She answered on the third ring.

"What? I told you not to call me. I spoke to Ira and he told me you shouldn't call. I could get a court order, you know that? I should do that. I should get a court order to stop you calling me every day. What do you want?"

"How are the kids?"

"That's what you called me for? To know how the kids are!"

"I miss them, they're my kids too. Do they miss me?"

"They're grown up, Paul. That's how they are. And they visit you twice a week. It's a shame you didn't miss them so much when they were kids. This whole thing might have been different."

"You think so?" She didn't answer. "What about Saul?"

"He has a cold, he's droopy. He's lying on the sofa now watching the old cartoons."

"Which ones?"

"Bugs Bunny, and the Road Runner. Remember...?"

She trailed off but he didn't notice and spoke over her. "I love Bugs Bunny and the Road Runner. We used to watch them together, remember? We'd cuddle on the sofa with Saul between us. And laugh! I never get tired of them."

"He misses you."

"Rub Vicks into his feet. Then you put woolly socks on his feet and cover him on the sofa with a duvet. Give him ginger and honey."

"I know how to treat a cold, Paul."

"I miss him."

"He misses you too."

"How about you?" But he didn't give her time to answer and asked, "You seeing a lot of Ira?"

"Paul, don't start that again. He's our lawyer! I'm not seeing anybody! What about you? With your balls and dinners and all your fancy friends!"

"You know I don't attend those functions. I work. And when I'm not working, I work. I go home to my empty house, and I work."

"I remember." It was only partly a criticism. "If only you hadn't worked so much."

"Time," he said and sighed, about to unveil his newly crafted phrase, but thought better of it, lest it be taken as a veiled recrimination, and instead crafted a new one: "It makes us all wise, but always too late."

"You always had a way with words."

"I'll be retiring soon."

"Maybe you could come for lunch, Sunday. Today's Friday. That would be the day after tomorrow."

"I know when Sunday is. Will Ira be there?"

"No, for heaven's sake!"

"That would be nice. I miss you, Ruth."

"I know."

"Not just the kids."

"I know."

"Us, you, me, the kids. The family. It's not right."

"I know. You have to stop now. Come for lunch."

She hung up and he sat and wept for a few minutes in silence. When he had stilled the spasms of grief in his belly he dried his eyes with his neatly folded handkerchief, collected his briefcase and stepped out of his office and into his secretary's office. She looked up at him and he paused in front of her desk.

"I have some things to attend to, Alice. I'll have my phone switched off for a couple of hours. After that you can find me at home." He was about to leave but hesitated a moment, then smiled. "Except Sunday. Sunday I'll be having lunch with my wife."

Alice grinned. "Oh, Colonel, is that a good sign?"

"It may be, Alice, wish me luck."

Colonel Hirschfield took the elevator down to the parking garage, collected his nondescript 2019 Honda Accord and emerged onto International Drive NW. Despite the deep relationship between Israel and the United States, and the deep reliance the two nations had on each other, the Israeli Embassy was not with the other major embassies along the river on Reservoir Road, like the French and the Germans, or ostentatiously on Massachusetts Avenue, like the British. It was discretely tucked away up beside Soapstone Valley, along with the Embassies of Ethiopia, Pakistan and Bangladesh. Some friends you received in the back room or the kitchen, others you were seen out with at the opera or in fancy restaurants. It's what diplomacy is all about.

He made his way along Van Ness and south down Connecticut Avenue, and eventually found his way to the Target shopping mall on 14th Street in Colombia Heights. There he bought a burner phone and took a walk. It was a VoicePing P-one Android cell phone for seniors, otherwise known as a Dumb Phone. What he liked best about it was that it did not have a touchscreen. While he walked he lamented the stupidity of the new age, and dialed a number he'd memorized; a number at the White House. It was answered immediately.

"Who is this and how did you get this number?"

"Jerry! Is that a way to greet an old friend?"

"Jesus, Paul! What the hell are you playing at? You can't —! And what's this number?"

He spoke fast, in a low voice, and Paul could visualize him moving quickly away from any people he had nearby.

"What's the matter, Jerry? You become suddenly anti-Semitic? You don't want people to know you're talking to Israeli Intelligence?"

"Come on, cut it out! What do you want, Paul?"

"I want to talk to my old friend, Jerry, security advisor to the president, who did such a superb job on the recent suit-case bomb crisis."

He spoke as though through clenched teeth. "I told you that is going to take time."

Paul sighed. He had reached Park Road and turned left toward 16th Street. "See, here's the thing, Jerry. I don't have a lot of time. Time is like patience," he said, telling himself he had come up with another nice line about time, "the more you use it, the less you have of it. And that applies to you and me both, Jerry."

"*I just haven't got that kind of money available right now!*" His voice was a savage whisper.

The colonel crossed Hyatt Place at the pedestrian crossing, carefully checking in both directions before stepping onto the blacktop.

"That's OK," he said. "I have to admit that my conscience has been causing me trouble. I am basically a good man with good values. But I am tired! I feel I am getting old, you know? So I thought it would be a good idea to secure an early retirement with a million bucks in the bank—"

"You said five hundred grand!"

"I know, but that's the way it goes, you see? Now you've said you're not going to pay, so I am free to fantasize! What's the difference? You're not going to pay anyway, right?" He laughed. "But in any case, like I was saying, it's a relief anyway because my conscience was troubling me. I should not let a bastard like you get away. At least, if I pass my information on to the CIA, their Special Activities Department will know what to do with you."

"No, now slow down, Paul! I didn't say I wouldn't pay!"

"You disgust me, Jerry. How many people died in Silicon Valley? Five thousand people? Women, children, old, young, killed in the most horrific way. And how much were you paid to facilitate that?"

"Paul, please—"

"No, you're right. I would rather look at my face in the morning knowing I had reported you, than look at my bank account knowing you were free."

"All right! All right!"

"I am going to have a nice weekend with my family, Jerry. And Monday morning, my first order of business when I sit down at my desk, will be to call the director of the CIA."

"Paul! Stop! This very afternoon you will have your five hundred grand—"

"One million bucks, Jerry. And if you procrastinate again it will be one and a half. Do it today. I'll check my account when I get home." He hung up and smiled, and muttered quietly to himself, "And then I'll call the CIA, you spineless traitor."

He removed the SIM card from the cell as he made his way back toward the shopping mall. As he walked he folded it in half a few times until it tore, dropped one piece in a trash can and dropped the other down a drain. The phone he slipped in his pocket, intending to incinerate it in the furnace in his basement of his house.

At home on Warren Street NW he left his car out front in the shade of the plane tree and made his way up two flights of stone steps to his redbrick porch, counting them as he had twice every day for the past ten years: seven in the first flight, seven in the second. And, as he had done twice a day for the past ten years, he joked to himself, "Still all there."

He closed the door on the bright sunshine and inhaled the cool, shady peace of his hallway. Six months ago the silence had startled and depressed him every time he got home. Now he had grown used to it and told himself it was one of the few things about being single he would miss if Ruth ever came back to him. The blessed silence.

He made his way to the drawing room and opened the French doors onto the backyard, where three steps led down to his patio. There was a patch of sun at the end by the red roses that made the green stand out, vibrant. He could smell the sweetness of the roses on the air. He went inside and mixed himself a Beefeater and tonic, with plenty of ice and lemon, and as he was about to descend the steps to his patio, his old-fashioned house phone rang. He gave God a baleful look, shook his head and sat on the sofa by the phone.

"Hello, this is Colonel Paul Hirschfield speaking."

The voice on the other end, pretty and feminine,

laughed. "Paul, do you seriously always answer the phone like that?"

"Oh," he said without much enthusiasm, "hello. Yes, I do. There was nothing wrong with it when my parents taught me to do it, and there's nothing wrong with it now."

"You're a rare treasure. Listen, Paul, have you thought about what we talked about?"

"No, I have thought about what you talked about, and I am afraid my answer is the same as it was then—"

She interrupted him. "Paul, you don't realize how important this is for me. It could swing everything. All I need is a word in his ear. He listens to you, he respects you—"

It was Paul's turn to interrupt. "Everyone in Washington listens to me and respects me. You listen to me and respect me. You know why? Because I have integrity. Because I give good advice. Because I am honest. And what you are asking me to do, Minnie, is dishonest."

"It's not dishonest! It's just..."

She trailed off and he said, "And *that's* dishonest. Telling yourself a thing is not dishonest when you know damn well it is. You're trying to walk a tightrope, Minnie, and it can't be walked. You want to court Arab oil and Jewish bankers, and you are going to end up getting badly hurt. If I go to Ben and tell him, I think you should endorse what Minnie is trying to do, I will lose all my credibility and all his trust. Because what you want to do does not benefit Israel, and it sure as hell does not benefit the United States."

"I've always thought of you as an uncle, Paul, one of the family. You know that."

"And I have always tried to teach you the values my

parents taught me when I was a kid. I know it hasn't been easy for you without your parents' guidance, but you have to hold fast to the righteous path."

"I'm sorry, Paul. I shouldn't have asked."

"Forget it. It's this town. Everybody is crazy for power. But my father, God rest him, drummed it into me every day of my childhood: 'Paul,' he'd say, 'power at any price is not power at all. It's slavery!'"

"I know, Paul, he was a wise man."

"OK, Minnie. We should get together soon. It's been too long. You've been busy, I've been busy. But you should come for lunch. Not this weekend 'cause I'm going over to Ruth's for lunch!"

"No kidding! Is this a sign of things to come?"

"Oh, I hope so, kiddo. I miss 'em so much, I can't tell you."

"I bet you do. Hell! *I* miss her and I'm not even married to her!"

"Yeah, I know, everybody loves her. Trouble is, she's tired of me. And that is one thing you can't do anything about."

"Give her time. She might come around. I think she still loves you, Paul."

He saw his hand shaking and fought to control his voice. "No, she feels sorry for me. But she's with Ira now. It's over, and to tell you the truth, Minnie, I'm about ready to move on."

"You got anyone in mind, you old dawg?"

"No, but I'm looking, and that's a good sign, right?"

They both laughed, promised to stay in touch and get together soon and he hung up.

He sat for a long time staring at the blank TV screen opposite. Eventually he blinked and realized he was still holding his gin and tonic. He placed it untouched on the lamp table beside the sofa and stood. He made his way up the stairs, crossed the broad landing and went into the matrimonial bedroom. He opened the top drawer in his nightstand and extracted a Sig Sauer Tacops P226, rammed in a magazine and went downstairs again. There he half closed the drapes, sat in the armchair in the corner of the room, beside the French doors, pulled over his gin and tonic and drained half of it.

He laid the semi-automatic on his lap and stared at it for a long while. When he looked at his drink again the ice cubes had all but melted. He drained what was left, closed his eyes and tried to steady his nerves. He had killed more than once in his life, on active duty. This would be just the same...just the same. Just point the gun in the right direction and pull the trigger.

Scan the QR code below to purchase EXECUTIVE ORDER.
Or go to: righthouse.com/executive-order

NOTES

PROLOGUE

1. 1,945 miles

CHAPTER 6

1. Punkt Propuska Brest Terespol

CHAPTER 12

1. Bunny

CHAPTER 14

1. Americans! Always with their guns!

CHAPTER 15

1. Beloved
2. Beloved mother

CHAPTER 16

1. The guilty act

CHAPTER 1

1. See *Russian Roulette*
2. See *Russian Roulette*